A DISPOSABLE MAN

A Tom Darby Adventure

By Dan L. Hollifield

Three Ravens Publishing
Chickamauga, GA USA

A DISPOSABLE MAN By Dan L. Hollifield
Published by Black Anvil – Blue Rose Press, an imprint of Three Ravens Publishing

threeravenspublishing@gmail.com
P O Box 851, Chickamauga, GA 30707
https://www.threeravenspublishing.com

Credits:
A DISPOSABLE MAN was written by Dan L. Hollifield
A DISPOSABLE MAN by: Dan L. Hollifield / Three Ravens Publishing – 1st edition, 2025

Edited by: Karin Harris

Ebook ISBN: 978-1-966507-14-7
Trade Paperback ISBN: 978-1-966507-15-4

Table of Contents

"The Author reserves the right to have a better idea"—
Larry Niven

If in any way this work diverges from an earlier,
connected work, see the above quote—Dan L. Hollifield

Dedication

To all my family and friends, my readers, my convention friends, my Mother, and most especially my Beloved Lindsey and our children. Thank you all for your support and for believing in me.

And as always, for Daddy…

Dan

(Once There Was) A Disposable Man...

I was having that damn nightmare again… My fighter jet had lost one wing, was on fire, and I was about 90 seconds from becoming a dead man. Funny how they say your whole life flashes before your eyes just before you're about to die. I was too busy trying to LIVE to notice that.

I wasted a lot of time in my young life before I managed to lie my way into the Army. From there, I got into the Air Corps and never looked back. Not even getting drafted by the spooks to fly camera missions behind the Iron Curtain was too bad a deal. Working for the spooks on the ground? That was bad, Sport. Real bad.

I rode the crash almost all the way to the ground before I tripped the ejector seat. Almost left it too late, but I had to make sure my plane wouldn't nosedive into the Korean village below. It wasn't easy clearing the flaming wreck, but somehow, I managed it. Must have been all the training. What was my first impression of Korea? The ground is *damned* hard, that's what. Still, five to one odds—and I was the only survivor? They don't make MIG pilots like they used to. No one'll ever believe that I got all five of them before I got shot down. Well, they asked for it.

Awareness slowly swims back, as if from a long distance. Every muscle of my body hurts, but I don't feel the sting of broken bones. I feel cold, damp brickwork against my bare back. I'm standing, after a fashion. I can hear water dripping not too very far away. I smell dust, and mud, and filth like an outhouse on a Summer's day. I can't move. My arms and legs are restrained. My armpits hurt like hell. I'm guessing that I'm strapped to a wall or something and that I'd been hanging there like a piece of meat before I came to. Bright light in my eyes as I blink them over and over again, attempting to see my surroundings. Through dazzled eyes I can make out the barest glimmer of some person standing between me and the spotlight. My head is killing me, and I feel like I'm going to puke. Possible concussion, then.

I'd gladly kill whoever it is that pointed that damn light in my face. But if they offered me a glass of water, I might decide to let them live. Red... Whoever it is that's in front of me is wearing red. With curves... My torturer is a woman, wearing some sort of Chinese silk dress. Blinking to clear the film from my eyes I can finally see a few details. The spotlight behind her makes her long hair look blonde. Too tall to be Asian. Desecrated that dress to show off her wide hips. I'm guessing that dress was worth more than my Saber jet was—before she took a pair of scissors to the dress, I mean.

Chinese silk, maybe 150 years old. Dress has patterns on it, but I can't make them out for the glare. I can see her feet clearly 'cause of the angle of the light. Red toenail polish, not bound feet but normal. Tall girl, too tall to be Asian. Western traitor, then. Even squinting I can't see her face because of the spotlight in my eyes. I cough and try to stand up straighter against my restraints. I can feel the rough texture of the bricks against my butt. So they'd stripped me naked, then. Probably trying to humiliate me, demoralize me, make it easier for them to question me. Fat chance...

"Hunh," I cough again. "Where am I THIS time?' I ask. My voice sounds like I haven't used it in a long time.

"A prisoner, due for summary execution," she says. "But if you answer our questions, you may yet live to see another dawn."

Her accent, French but tutored in English by someone British. There's something about the letter R that French people just can't disguise no matter how many English lessons they take. Long way from home, Honey. What are you doing in Korea? Why are you interrogating me instead of the enemy military?

"Crank the lights down a hair, will you?" I asked. "My head is still splitting from the plane crash. Or I could just puke on your shoes, if you like."

"Cretin!" she says. Yeah, French. A real Britt would have called me an arsehole, or something similar. Time to demonstrate that I'm not going to be easy to break.

"Mamzelle," I said. "I'm not the one stuck half a world away from my home, workin' for the Commies. You wanna do us both a favor and get to the point before I die of *old age*?"

Shocked silence. I guess my opening salvo hit pretty close to the mark. She ought to recover any minute now, though—

"Silence!" she shouted.

"How'd you expect me to answer questions if I stay silent, Honey?" I goaded her. But I spoiled the witticism by coughing again. My mouth was watering enough to fill a bucket in quick order. I knew I was gonna puke really soon. Sure enough, I lost all the advantages I'd gained so far by hurling whatever was left of my last meal all over the floor in front of my bare feet. Felt like I retched for hours, but it couldn't have been even a minute. Well, maybe two minutes. But the light dimmed a little.

Enough so that I could see her now. Nice figure, blonde hair, superior smirk on her face. Too bad, she'd have been really attractive without that Nazi snarl. Yeah, wrong war, so what? I'm in Korea, not Germany. I know, so sue me. At least the smell of my own vomit was enough to kick my concussed brain into a higher gear. And just then they hit me with water from a fire hose. Low pressure, not like a real fire hose. At least it washed my stink away while it prompted me further awake. Time to seize the high ground, I think.

"Lady, I have been tortured by experts. I know the drill. I know every question you've been ordered to ask me. Can we stop with the amateur hour and get with the program? I'm bored, I'm tired, I'm concussed, I'm naked and chained to a wall, and you have all the subtlety of the Orient Express running into a cow on the train tracks. I don't rate *you* very highly at all. I wake up from crashing my plane after shooting down half a dozen MIGs, and your *owner* thinks that the sight of your hips and tits is enough to make me babble all the secrets you *think* I know? Either cut me down and take me to your boss, or just shoot me, *please*. But put your ego aside and quit playing to whoever is watching you try and question me! Your skills are *pitiful*."

She cussed me out, in French, for at least three minutes. As far as I could tell, she didn't repeat herself once. Theory about her origins is confirmed. Not only was she French, but very High Class, so to speak. Old Money family— Aristocrats, probably Daddy lost all the family's money backing the wrong army in WWII, I'd bet. The accent wasn't familiar, but then I stopped listening when she was saying how much she'd enjoy watching me— It was either me getting shot or me getting my balls cut off, I couldn't tell. My French was a little rusty.

"I think your owners have more to say about it than you," I said once she ran out of steam. "So take me to them before I nod off from boredom. Amateur..." Yeah, I was trying to piss her off. So sue me. You get tied naked to a wall after crashing a fighter jet and see how good a mood you're in. I'm only human, after all.

And that's about the point in this recurring nightmare where I usually wake up. Sometimes I'm screaming, sometimes I'm just sweating with fear. I don't know why this dream always comes back. Sure, the basic scene really happened. Part of my time in Korea that I don't want to remember. I don't know why the dream-me talks with my real, old-man voice, either. Back when I got myself captured—Hell, I was barely past seventeen. Thanks to a providential fire in the county courthouse when I was about ten, there weren't any records to prevent me from claiming I was old enough to enlist when the war started. I made it through boot camp without giving myself away. I managed to do well enough on some tests to get me into the Air Corps. I wound up flying a Saber jet, eventually.

I never shot down six MIGs in one go, though. It was only two, and I didn't even get to shoot at the second one. Poor kid must have been as green as I was. We both turned the wrong way at the same time and he ripped through my left wing. I managed to ride the damn thing down far enough to miss a village we'd been over, then popped my ejector seat. I saw him fireball into a hillside as I came down. He never had a chance to eject. I must have been too close to the ground when I pulled the lever. I hit the ground pretty hard. Knocked myself out. I'd been captured while I was unconscious. Some Chi-com unit was close enough to find me before I had time to come to.

Yeah, I was tied up and about to be interrogated when I did wake up. Wasn't any woman there, though. It was an officer, maybe North Korean, maybe Chinese--big and burly and mad as hell at me. He threatened me with a lot of stuff he never got around to doing. Most of the torture I did get was psychological, not physical. Sleep deprivation, water hoses, lack of food. Oh, he had a table loaded with improvised stuff he'd roll out to show me. C-clamps, knives, a branding iron, splinters of wood, even a whip made from a frayed electrical cord. Mostly he just had a couple of grunts slap me around a bit while he shouted questions. I passed out a lot. I couldn't give him much intel, though. Hell, I didn't know much anyway.

In between beatings I'd make up a load of hogwash about whatever he seemed to be interested in. That went on for about two weeks before I got a lucky break. Well, it was lucky for me, anyway. The camp I was being held in got shelled. Killed the Commies and busted the stone walls of the building they had me locked up in. I wasn't tied up right then, or I'd probably just starved to death before I could get out of the restraints. When the shelling stopped, I got out and took a quick look around. I managed to find a few scraps of food in what was left of their mess tent. I scavenged corpses for a couple of pistols and some ammo. Found a canteen full of water, too. By nightfall I'd hightailed it out of the area, headed back towards our side of the line. I got some help from a couple of farms along the way. Some more food, water, a blanket that didn't have too many fleas.

None of the natives wanted to kill me for being American. That was weird, but I was thankful for it.

Eventually, a week or so later, I made it as far as a MASH unit that was packing up to bug out. They checked me out and put me on one of their trucks. I kept fading in and out. I finally woke up still strapped to a stretcher, IV stuck in my arm, being unloaded at their new camp site. After a few days their CO managed to get a transport lined up for me. I got shipped out back to my airbase. Everybody kept telling me I was lucky to be alive. I didn't think they were going to let me fly again, though. I thought they were going to pin a medal on me and ship me back to West Virginia. Probably make me pay for the damn jet, too. Then the Spooks showed up.

The company Shrink came in one day to tell me I was being released. He also told me I had some high-powered visitors that wanted me to double-time it over to the Commander's office. When I got there, they were all glad-handing me and congratulating me on walking out of that mess. Asked me if I wanted to keep serving my country, or did I want to turn tail and ship out for home. One of them kept acting like I'd turned traitor and gave the Commies everything they wanted. The other two played nice-nice. I wasn't green enough to fall for either side, but I told them I wanted back in a plane. I had nothing to go home to except to try and turn a rocky hillside into a farm. That's what I ran away from in the first place, so I didn't really want to go back. After a while they made me an offer. Not combat, but photo recon. They wanted me to join the Spooks. So, I did. Got me back into a jet, anyway. I got a promotion out of the deal, too.

At first they had me flying over targets after combat, to photo the results. After a while, they sent me out to find new targets. One guy, my official handler, seemed to have a problem with his bosses. I called him Joe, even though that wasn't his real name. Seems Joe's superiors had a hard-on to get hold of a working MIG. From what he said, and I figured out more from what he *didn't* say, his bosses were constantly bustin' his chops about findin', and stealin', the newest model MIG the spooks could locate.

I'd been flying recon for Joe for about a year by then. Joe and I went out to the Officer's Club one evening—that didn't happen often—and he laid it on the line for me. One of my recent missions had me passing over a little airstrip our boys had pushed pretty close to. There was a single MIG working out of that strip. A fairly new one, Joe said. All the latest bells and whistles, with just a bare minimum ground crew and a couple of pilots based there. The little airstrip's security looked to be mostly a platoon of locals and a pair of Ruskies as a ground crew for the jet.

Joe wanted to put together a ground team to pull off a strike on that strip and capture that MIG. But he needed a pilot to fly it back so our Spooks could take it apart and see what made it tick. The timing was really tight. The Commies would pull the fighter out of there if our forces got too close, and we were just about too close already. He could give me a day and a half to sit in the cockpit of a crashed MIG that the Spooks had recovered from somewhere. Did I think I could puzzle out enough from a wrecked piece of junk to get a working MIG into the air and bring it home? We talked half the night about it. He was buying the beer. Wasn't good beer, but it was cold, so I kept listening. Sometimes I'd even ask an intelligent question.

I woke up the next morning with a headache, and reported for duty. Joe got a jeep and we went to see the remains of the MIG the Spooks had. I could smell the smoke before I got within ten feet of it. Wasn't much to look at, but it was a cockpit and a few feet of the thing's nose. There was blood on the instrument panel, and soot, and some other stuff I didn't want to know what it was. I took a bucket and some rags and cleaned it up enough to read the labels on the instruments. Joe had a couple of pages of Russian translations of what the labels were supposed to mean. Some of the switches and dials were in odd positions, but within a couple of hours I could tell what was supposed to be what. A jet is a jet, and I figured that if I could get the engines started, I could take off and land without too much trouble. After a couple of days practice with the wreckage, Joe and I joined up late one afternoon with about thirty guys he'd rounded up to tiptoe up to that airstrip and give me a chance to fire that mother up.

Over half of them were hard cases. Discipline problems—insubordination, striking an officer, drunk on duty, fights in the bar, and worse. Over the past year, all of those had been pulled out of stockades all over the place, then sent here and promised their charges would be dropped if they came back alive. The rest were borderline crazy. Some of them had lost close friends in combat and wanted revenge. Some of them just plain enjoyed combat. The unit CO that Joe hand-picked to ride herd over this bunch of gallows-fruit was probably the only man in the whole Army who was tougher than they were.

Captain Robert Teacher, Joe called him Bad Bob, the men called him Teach. I called him Sir when officers were around—and in front of his unit. He told me to call him Teach when we were in the bar, or bein' informal-like. It only took one fight for the unit to learn Teach wasn't anyone they wanted to cross. I hear the guy only spent a few weeks in the med unit after Teach beat the crap out of him for swinging on him. I had a week to get to know them better and train alongside them before the mission was given a "go." I heard from Teach that the Base Commander called the unit the Untouchables. I got the impression that the Commander would have gladly stood the entire unit up before a firing squad if it weren't for whatever rank Joe held. The CO was the CO, but sometimes Joe told him what to do. Neither of them liked each other very much. You figure out the power struggle that implied, I didn't have time. I had a commie fighter jet to steal.

So—we got trucked out to the badlands in the middle of the night. We left the vehicles behind and crept up on the airstrip about two days later. We watched the MIG come back from a mission just before dark on the second day. I climbed a tree and watched through my binoculars as the jet was refueled and reloaded with a couple of missiles and a crate of machine gun rounds. Joe was there with Teach and Teach's unit. We finalized the plan, and waited until full dark. There couldn't have been more than a dozen Commies manning the airstrip. Joe wanted Teach to capture the two pilots, if possible. Other than that, the kid gloves were off. The unit would storm the strip, kill everyone except for the pilots, and give me time to steal the bird. If possible, that is. Like I said, we waited and watched their ground crew and pilots refuel the jet. Then we waited some more.

Once it was full dark, we moved out into our final positions. The airstrip had a couple of wooden shacks thrown together off under the trees at the far end. One was a barracks, the other was a bar. There was also a tent that was obviously the mechanics' little kingdom. The strip ended in a drop-off where the MIG would leap into the air. Must have been a hundred feet or more from the end of the strip to the valley below. If I didn't have the speed up high enough when I hit the end of the strip, I'd make a nice campfire at the bottom of the cliff.

Teach had the men move closer, slowly, carefully. Joe stayed by my side the whole time. He was careful to keep me back from the fighting. Don't know if he thought I'd chicken out and run away, or if he was willing to die to keep me safe to steal the jet. Maybe I'll never know. Maybe I never want to know. Right about then Teach blew a whistle, and Hell came to Korea.

The first volley of rifle fire took out the mechanics in their tent. Splinters flew off of the barracks and bar sheds as the guys pelted up close. There were a few rounds torched off from the bar, but that stopped when the guys turned the place into a free-fire zone. Wasn't much like a war. It was more like murder. Joe told me later that one of the pilots was captured, wounded but alive. None of the rest of those poor bastards made it out alive.

We only lost seven men from the unit as the Commies returned fire. They had machine guns. They hosed our guys down like so many mad dogs. It was only the darkness that saved the rest of us. Once the hellfire ended, Joe slapped me on the shoulder and told me to go do my job. I looked him in the eyes as best I could in the dark. I told him to get the guys home or die trying. They earned it, and he'd better keep his promises. He told me to shut the hell up and get that bird in the air. I ran towards the MIG and managed to not get shot by my own team.

Once I found the ladder and climbed into the cockpit, I realized that there wasn't anyone to unhook the ladder so I could close the canopy. I solved that problem by a lift and shove that sent the ladder to the dirt. I buttoned up the cockpit and started flipping switches by feel. I heard the compressor catch and felt the turbine start to spin. Once I knew I had everything running fast enough, I fed the torch some gas. The engine coughed twice before it lit. I found the light switches and flipped them with one hand while I shoved the throttle to the firewall with the other.

After about two of the longest seconds of my life, the MIG climbed over the wheel chocks that I'd forgotten to remove. I held the brakes as long as I could stand while the engine roared up to speed. Once I let them go, the stupid thing seemed to crawl towards the end of the runway. I kept pushing the throttle, even though it was already full up, all the way down the strip. I figured out how to angle the flaps just before I ran out of runway. The beast was falling towards the base of the cliff when I pulled back on the stick and forced her to climb into the sky. I switched off all the lights except for the instruments as I clawed my way up into the night.

The stupid jet was bucking and twisting like a wild horse being broken to the saddle for the first time. Clearly, I wasn't anywhere near as skilled as I'd been bragging that I was. Somehow, I managed to wrestle the junk heap into the sky and set a course for our side of the line. I found the switch to retract the landing gear, and the flight got a little less bumpy. The MIG smoothed out a bit further once I had more of the speed, I needed to get the hell out of Dodge. Once I was at speed and on course, I smiled to myself.

"This ain't so bad," I said. "Unless this piece of shit is harder to land than it was to lift, I'm in the clear. What can go wrong?"

Tracer bullets streaked past me in the darkness.

"When am I ever going to learn to keep my mouth shut?" I shouted as I worked the stick back and forth trying to confuse whoever it was shooting at me. If they got a missile lock with a heat seeker, I was going to be a dead man really quickly. Even a lucky burst with their machine guns would make this a really short escape.

I dove, jinking the beast back and forth the whole way. I saw what looked like a river below me. I knew that if I got down that low I'd become an easy target. The trees on the river banks would keep me from dodging effectively, so I reached for the switch that released chaff to confuse my attacker's radar lock. Once the chaff was away, I popped a flair to confuse their heat seekers and pulled the stick back all the way. Within moments I was as high as the bird would go without stalling.

The ground lit up beneath me as the enemy's missiles detonated where I was a few minutes ago. If they were any good, and I just knew they had to be, they'd figure out what I did and be climbing up my ass within seconds. So I popped another flair and some more chaff and dove towards the river. I thought the wings were going to rip off the beast before I could level out. I was scared out of my mind and cussing a blue streak when suddenly I remembered something.

I remembered West Virginia. Steep hills and narrow, twisting roads. I remembered being five years old and riding shotgun with Grandpa Loomis on a 'shine run to Knoxville. The cops were close behind, lights and sirens blasting out. Sometimes the road would be straight enough for a cop to get a shot off at the old Packard Grandpa and Uncle Johnny had rebuilt from junk. I remembered Grandpa cussing when his wing mirror shattered from a lucky shot from the cop car closest behind us. I remembered what Grandpa did when he saw a dirt road up ahead.

I jerked the stick to the left and banked the beast into the tightest turn I could make it manage. I leveled it out and just barely cleared the tree tops at the edge of the river, then I shoved the stick right and got back on course for the base. I could just barely make out the trees below me. I kept twisting the stick from side to side, left, right, left, pull back and hop a ridge, then back down and to the left again, then right to follow another ridge towards home. I was burning way too much gas. Even with a full tank I was going to be lucky if I managed to have enough left to land. Assuming that I made it all the way to the base before running the tanks dry.

Two more explosions from missiles, wide of the mark, one to my left and one to my right. Whoever was chasing me was good, but I could hear Grandpa Loomis in the back of my mind. He was singing Amazing Grace and driving like a madman. We shot past three paved roads that led off the dirt road before he slung the big black Packard into a tight turn onto a logging trail that I just barely had time to see. His thin, reedy voice never missed a word of the hymn. I chanced a look at the speedometer as we hurtled through the narrow track between the pines. We were doing 95 on a road that no one should have been able to navigate at 25.

I remembered Grandpa telling me "I think we lost that bluenose, for now. If I remember right, there's a bridge up ahead. If we make it over that, we're just a hop, skip, and a jump from the road that'll get us into Knoxville. You all right, Tommy Boy?"

"I'm scared, Paw-Paw, but I trust you," I remember saying to him.

"Good boy," he said. "Scared ain't nothin' but a feelin' an' feelin's can't kill you. Just trust in the Lord and do whatever it takes to get the job done..."

I drew strength from that memory of my Paw-Paw, and jerked that jet all over the sky. Somewhere over the Korean hills, I saw the brightest flash of light yet. My enemy had failed to counter my random turns and rammed his plane into the ground. I chanced a quick loop to see if there was anyone else on my back trail.

Nothing, not a sign, so I leveled back out and took a straight path back to base. That stupid Russian jet was still bucking and shaking like I'd done it a damage. My teeth were rattling. But I could see the lights of the airstrip I wanted, just up ahead. Now all I had to do was make the delivery. Land this beast and turn it over to Joe and his Spooks.

"Knoxville," I whispered. "Here I come... Thank you, Paw-Paw." About fifteen minutes later, the runway of my target base was right there beneath me. I pulled the throttles back, set the flaps, and put that piece of junk on the ground. Spooks met me in the airstrip I'd landed on, then hustled me away for what seemed like months of debriefing. Longest week of my life, I'll tell you.

After that, I was allowed to go back to photo recon duty. But word must have gotten around, somehow. I wound up getting better jets for my missions, for one thing. For another, I noticed that the higher ranks treated me with a little more respect.

Eventually, the war ended but then the spooks wanted me full-time. Cold War, they called it. Whatever. As long as I could keep flyin', I wasn't bothered much by changin' assignments. I ran into Joe from time to time. Seems he got promoted, too. Then the Russians managed to shoot down a U-2 while it was actually on a photo recon mission.

Everything changed and I got reassigned again. Mostly ground-side, for a long while. That wasn't as much fun as you'd think. Then I got to fly again, for the spooks, when they replaced the U-2 with something way better. The spooks called it the A-12. I called it the Beast. I flew a dozen missions in the Beast, then it got retired in favor of the latest model, the SR-71 Blackbird. I got forced into ground-side missions at the same time. I never got to fly an SR-71. I lost out on that. But I did get to fly an SMT-42 Nightbird once, but I'm getting ahead of myself…

On The Wings Of An Angel

"Occasionally, I have to make deliveries…"
— Tom Darby

I only ever flew a U-2 once, and it wasn't a photo-recon mission. I was assigned to be a delivery boy, instead. It seems that there was a vital mission that needed new, special cameras. The Powers That Be had refitted a U2 with these improved cameras, Stateside, and now they wanted the plane delivered to whoever was going to fly the mission—somewhere out in the field.

I was enjoying a weekend leave in California at the time. On Sunday afternoon, the spooks sent a couple of MPs to track me down and take me back to base. The Base Commander was waiting when I got hustled into his office. As soon as I saw him, I figured he had to be pissed off about having to come to the office on a Sunday. I was pretty sure he was going to take it out on *me*.

"Thank you, gentlemen," he said to the MPs as I stood at attention. "Dismissed…" he added, looking at them as if they were a pair of housecats that'd just delivered a skunk to his office. "Sit," he ordered me as the door closed behind the MPs. I sat.

"Darby," he began. "Sorry to cut your leave short. But I have been ordered to get you—somewhere—before dawn tomorrow, for a special assignment."

Yes sir," I replied. "But the MPs didn't let me have time to pay my bill. I owe Rosie for an overnighter with her best pair of girls—"

"Your bill has been paid," he said. "Your pay has been docked for the full amount. But as I understand, this mission has enough bonuses attached to keep you from going without a payday for the next month. Miss Rosie is not unknown to the staff here. There's special paperwork to deal with, ahem, this kind of situation." He looked just a hair embarrassed to admit that, but then he changed the subject. "There's something your 'handlers' need you to do, something you're evidently uniquely suited for doing, and I've been assigned to get you to—wherever it is they need you."

"*Thank you*, sir. Rosie is NOT someone I want mad at me! What's the drill?"

"At 04:30 tomorrow, there will be a transport here to take you to your next assignment. I suggest you return to the BOQ and shower, then get as much sleep as you can before then. Quite frankly, you smell like a whorehouse on payday, even from here."

"Sorry sir," I said. "I'll attend to that ASAP. Is there anything else?"

"Just out of curiosity," he replied. "And strictly off the record. Which two girls?"

"Kitty and Doris," I said, refusing to blush.

"Well," he replied. "If nothing else, you have excellent taste. You ought to be able to sleep well enough after that. Um, you have a thing for older women?"

"Sir," I said carefully. "Between the two of them they have over 80 years of experience in—what they do. A boy like me needs to learn from experts, sir. I haven't much experience in ah, *that* sort of advanced education. If I live long enough to get married, I don't want my wife to feel like I'm, um, not good enough to wait for while I'm off on a mission."

"Smart boy," he replied. "But remember," he added. "Once you have a wife to come home to, 'further education" may be detrimental to domestic bliss."

"SIR! Yes Sir! Daddy said the same thing to me," I said.

"Sounds like a wise man," he said. "Take it to heart and maybe you won't be a disappointment to your future wife. Dismissed."

"Thank you, Sir."

So, I went to my quarters, got cleaned up and went straight to bed. I set my alarm for 03:00 so I'd have a chance for another quick shower and a quicker run to the mess hall before I needed to get on my transport. Whatever it was the spooks wanted me to do, I'd already learned, long ago, that my breakfast was *really* low on their list of priorities.

The next morning, I got a very quick, very hot shower to supplement the longer one I'd taken the afternoon before. I managed to make it to the mess hall and grab half a dozen biscuits, sausage patties, a huge pile of scrambled eggs, and some diced potatoes. Even managed a ladle of gravy for right then. I ate three of the biscuits and sausage, the gravy, and the potatoes—washing that down with three cups of strong black coffee before running to meet the jeep that was supposed to take me to my transport.

The passenger plane I met, and boarded, was a little 12-seater, twin engine jet with external fuel tanks strapped to each wing. As I climbed the boarding ladder, I noticed the jet's windows were painted black. When you're working for spooks, that ain't a good sign. Wherever I was going, sightseeing along the route was not permitted, so, someplace secret, then.

I was the only passenger. The pilot and co-pilot waited just long enough for me to take a seat and strap in. Nobody said a word about my paper lunch bag with my remaining three sausage and egg biscuits or my thermos of coffee. Another long-ago lesson had been that in-flight meals were up to *me* to provide, once the spooks wanted me to go do something. Then we navigated over to the runway we were cleared to use, and the little jet screamed its way into the still-dark sky.

I was too nervous to try and get more sleep. I drank coffee and ate two more of my biscuits before we got wherever we were flying to. When we landed, it was still morning, but it was already hot as hell. I got off the plane carrying my remaining biscuit and the dregs of my coffee. I looked around and there was dry, flat ground, as far as I could see with mountains in the distance. A jeep was waiting for me. I got in and the driver wordlessly took off towards a set of low buildings in the distance. When we got to the buildings, there was a Staff Sergeant waiting for me. I got out of the jeep and the driver took off like a bat outta hell.

"If you'll follow me sir," the Sergeant said. "You have a briefing in seven minutes."

I saw a tumbleweed bounce past us, about half a football field away, driven towards the sunrise by a wind from the West. I had a fairly good guess as to where I was. "Where am I?" I asked anyway, on the off chance that I'd be permitted a little *informal* pre-flight briefing from the Sergeant.

"That's classified," he said. "But welcome to Dreamland. Let's get you to your briefing. Whatever questions you have clearance to have answered, are gonna be answered in there," he added, pointing to the low, sand-colored building we were standing outside.

"Let's go," I replied. "I hope there's more coffee…"

"Captain Darby, please take a seat," I was told as the Sergeant left me at the room where the briefing was supposed to happen. There were two guys in lab coats, an Air Force Major, and a Lieutenant that seemed to be some senior officer's secretary, already there when I arrived. "We've got a lot of ground to cover, and not a lot of time," the Major said.

"Coffee?" I asked.

"The urn is over there," the Lieutenant replied, pointing to the back, left corner of the room. "Drink too much though, and you'll need to wear a catheter for the mission."

Long flight to somewhere, I thought.

"Down to business?" The Major asked once I was back in a chair with a fresh cup of coffee.

"Yes, please," I replied.

"Captain Darby," said the Lieutenant. "We need you to deliver a U-2 for us. There is a specially qualified U-2 Pilot waiting at a base in the Middle East. *He* is assigned to fly this modified plane across—three enemy nations. Your job will be to get the plane to him in time for his recon to be on schedule. Think you're up to the assignment?"

I took a sip of my coffee, sat the cup of sub-standard, hot, brown, adulterated-water on the table. "Who will be shooting at me and how far do I have to go?" I asked. "Obviously, this base is either in Nevada or New Mexico. In order to reach anywhere *useful* to us in the Middle East I will need at least one in-flight refueling. Maybe two, depending on the route you assign me. U-2s are unarmed. I will have to outfly anything that gets shot at me or sent up to intercept me. It's just BARELY possible the Commies have something that could reach the normal service altitude of a U-2. Dunno. You're the experts. You tell me."

"We don't anticipate anyone being able to detect your flight or interfere with it in any way," said the Major.

"With all due respect, Major," I replied. "Your expectations are worth about as much to me as a sidewinder rocket packed with dog turds instead of explosives. I need a flight plan, a full report on any and every possible unfriendly along that route, I need to know the destination for delivery, and I need to know what sort of timetable I am expected to follow."

"You are insubordinate--" began the Lieutenant. I cut him off right there.

"Keeps me alive and allows me to complete missions successfully," I said. "It works. Don't knock it. Y'all want me to do this thing, then I need the proper intel."

A hidden door opened up in what I thought was a blank wall. A three-star General walked out. "We were told that you are the best," he said.

"I *am*," I replied. "But I can't operate at my best if I don't have all the intel I could possibly need to get the job done. It's your airplane, but it's my life. I'd like to know enough to protect both."

"You'll do," said the General. "Gentlemen, you are dismissed. Thank you. Please send in the mission specialists so the real briefing can begin. That will be all."

"I'm General Whitgar," he said when the room was empty of everyone but he and I. "The reports I have on you said that you had absolutely no respect for idiots, rank is meaningless to you, and despite those drawbacks, you're the best there is at anything we ask you to do."

"Fair enough," I said. "And that's true as far as it goes. Closer to the mark to say I don't respect chair-warmers who never *earned* their rank, but I don't *disrespect* anyone who knows what they're doing."

"We've got a U-2 outfitted with special cameras that no one has ever had before. We—*I*, need you to deliver the plane to an airfield in Kuwait, for one of our more experienced U-2 pilots to fly over Saudi Arabia, Turkey, Russia, China, and Southeast Asia. Can you do it?"

"In-flight refueling? I asked.

"East coast—off of Savannah Georgia, then again over North Africa. Stay the fuck away from Cuba, even if it means you have to fly through a hurricane."

"I can do that," I said.

"Then you're the man I need…" General Whitgar said.

"Then I leave at dawn?" I asked.

"You leave in 49 minutes. Finish your breakfast and go suit the fuck up," he said. "Good luck, son," he added. "Don't screw this up, Hot Shot. There's more riding on it than I'm allowed to tell you."

"Sir! Yes sir!" I said, as I stood and saluted. "Thank you for your trust, Sir," I added. The General left—through the ordinary door—and another MP showed up half a minute later to lead me to the ready room.

40 minutes later I was taking off and headed for Savannah…

The flight was uneventful. Inflight refueling was a cakewalk, both times. The weather was flawless all the way across the US. I met the first tanker about fifty miles off the Georgia coast. I threaded the needle with the refueling boom, took on a full load to top off my tanks, then made a gentle turn. In order to avoid Cuba, I flew northeast for a while, then turned East towards Tunisia. I refueled again just off the coast of Africa, then took a straight path to Kuwait. I must have crossed the most godforsaken path across the continent. Miles and miles of nothing but empty miles. Yeah, there was *some* greenery, but greenery meant people, so I skirted around it as best I was able. Stayed as high as I could, too.

Finally, I landed in the desert, miles and miles from Kuwait City. A ground crew surrounded the plane as soon as I dismounted. I turned Big Bird over to that US ground crew at some temporary base I *never* learned the name of, and got escorted by a pair of MPs straight to a C-47 to go home. Never got told—never asked, never knew—what the new cameras were supposed to look for, what or where the other pilot was supposed to photograph. Not my mission. I was just delivering a plane.

Coincidentally, a few months later, Gary Powers got shot down over Russia. That opened a huge can of worms. The spooks got spooked, in a manner of speaking. Luckily, America had an ace up her sleeve. Something new that had been in the works for a while. But the bugs hadn't been entirely ironed out, at the time. U2s got phased out, eventually. It took a while. Even made a come-back, later on, but their days were numbered just as soon as that Russian ground force got off one damned lucky shot. Maybe General Whitgar pulled some strings, maybe it was somebody else, but I got in on the ground floor when the new planes started flying real missions.

I got transferred to the A-12 program after that U2 delivery mission. I flew the Beast at three times the speed of sound at an altitude that was stupid crazy over Russia, China, and Southeast Asia for twelve missions over the next few years. I was in a rotation with several other pilots. Still can't name names, though. Still classified, as far as I know. I got surface to air missiles shot at me on five of those missions. Only once did a missile get within five miles of my position and altitude. I dodged and rammed the throttle home then, and found out what flying at damned close to *four* times the speed of sound felt like. Eventually, the A-12 program ended and the SR-71 program took over. I never got to fly an SR-71. Wish I had. From what I hear, the Sled was a dream machine. Leaked like a sieve until it got airborne and heated up a mite, but still—never came close to being shot down. Not ever.

After that, I was promoted again and transferred groundside. I didn't get to fly much after that. The only time that was memorable was when I had to steal an F-104G from an airfield in West Germany because my ground mission for the spooks went totally into the shitcan. I lost my entire team to the Commies. Somebody tumbled to what we were up to, and they got picked off, one by one. Only reason I escaped was that I can fly anything—and the Commies never expected me to try and steal one of their jets to get my ass back across the Berlin Wall. But that's a story for another day…

Catch A Falling Starfighter

"I think I would have preferred the firing squad…"
— Tom Darby.

Russian-controlled East Berlin was a totalitarian paradise. Everyone was controlled. Any act of rebellion or independence was answered with instant execution or imprisonment. Case in point, when I was assigned to a batch of spooks in East Germany in the '60s. Must have been early '60s 'cause JFK was still alive. I didn't even know what the team was after. I was just their extraction pilot, not a real spook. Never even figured out why I was ground-side with them instead of just meeting them on some back road somewhere with a cargo plane big enough for all six of them plus me.

Six weeks on the outskirts of Berlin and the entire team had either been captured, killed, or shipped off to Moscow to be tried in some kind of kangaroo court. Somehow, I'd evaded capture. But I was on my own, alone, behind the Iron Curtain. I had to get out of there before anyone on the team got tortured enough to give me up in order to make the pain stop.

Now look, I've been tortured by amateurs and experts alike. Once somebody reaches a certain point—different for everyone, I'm sure—they'd sell their own mothers or children to try and put a stop to it. I understand. Hell, I saw Mickey get picked up by a patrol as I was on my way to meet up with him. Right there on the street, in front of the café where we were supposed to meet. He was the last member of the team to be captured. Bobby was first, but he got off easy, they just shot him dead right there in that park we used for dead-drops. Well, he dropped dead all right. 7.63 Mauser bullet, right through his head. Buncha guys in heavy, gray coats shot him, and then toted him off like a sack of rotted potatoes. Brenda and Elsa were next—they just vanished. They were locals the team recruited, so I never found out if they just ran or got caught. Mack, Darren, Chuck, Artie, and Simon vanished in short order. Artie got in a hit-and-run with a black sedan. Kinda odd since he was on a freaking *sidewalk* at the time. Darren was poisoned—Simon told me there was a dart in his neck when he died. Then Simon got arrested half an hour after we'd last talked—when he told me about Darren. Mack and Chuck just disappeared. Never did find out what happened to them. Just, poof, and gone.

So, I'm alone behind the Wall. Matter of time before I get picked up or assassinated. And the only thing I could do was pray the Commies didn't know I was part of their, my friend's, team—yet. Only a matter of time. My advantages were pretty damn few. I knew where the team had stashed some gear they couldn't afford to carry around with them. My German and Russian language skills were the best I could manage, and I'd been assigned a different hotel than they had in order to distance myself from them. I knew the checkpoints across the border were impossible for a lone man. I'd been assigned some dinky Russian pistol instead of the Colt I favored—as part of my disguise. It wasn't a bad pistol, just really small. I had documents that purported to show that I was a German National, or a Russian for that matter, but I decided to toss the Russian papers in a trash can 'cause their records wouldn't have me in them under that name at all. I turned my hat brim down and flipped my raincoat collar up because of the light, spitting rain and plodded back towards my hotel at a nice, easy, totally unsuspicious pace. I stepped into a coffee house for a cup of something hot, black and warming that wasn't entirely disgusting—for European coffee. Once the rain slacked off to almost nothing, I left and wandered around at random—checking to see if I had picked up a tail. I didn't see anyone following me, so I went to a nightclub for a touch of the cheapest liquid courage my disguise would allow. Rotgut, really. But my language skills got polished as a side effect. A couple of hookers took an interest in me, but I told them I was broke and down on my luck, so eventually they went off in search of more suitable prey. Once I was sure no one was following me, I went back to my hotel to think. I hoped I could come up with a plan.

I sat there reading newspapers for two days. The only times I left the room was to get a meal and keep my disguise current by sticking to the routine I'd established for the past few weeks. I went to a couple of clubs, the regular café I'd been frequenting, an opera once—although I slept through most of it, and kept up appearances as best I could.

I was scared to death the whole time. I mean, seriously, I'd much rather have been in a fighter jet getting shot at in a dogfight than walk those streets. But I had an act to perform. Any deviation from the identity I'd adopted could give me away. It was a really frightening time, Sport. I hate working for spooks. I sincerely hate working for spooks. But there's nothing better for focusing the mind than being hyper aware of just how narrow a tightrope I'd been walking.

In my room, on the third day after the last of the team had been "ghosted," I read about something in one of the newspapers that gave me a glimmer of hope. Something about extra security at a nearby airport. I wondered why.

So I dug a bit deeper in some more papers, plus some gossip I overheard at my café, and found out that something weird was going on there. Some West German pilot had been forced down and his plane was forbidden for the locals to go see. Seems it was an American-designed plane, a single-seater fighter jet, no less. That detail was only in one early edition of one single paper. No later edition mentioned it, and neither did any other paper, but the gossip at the café hinted at it too. That told me that the Iron Curtain had come down well and truly hard on something the Russians didn't want the German public to know about. The game, as the saying goes, was afoot.

The next day I risked going to the old warehouse the team had stored their gear in. The stuff they couldn't afford to be caught with, I mean, and once I was sure no one was watching it, I broke in and grabbed a few choice items. I could only risk being seen with the briefcase my disguise had become known for, but I packed that sucker with everything I could stuff into it. My raincoat pockets, too. I even stashed a couple of packets of plastique under my hat. When I got back to my hotel room, I had three pistols within reach at all times. On my way up I had told the desk clerk and all the bellhops that I felt like I was coming down with something—from the rain and chill weather. I ordered some kind of hot soup from room service that night, and had coated my lips with beeswax and practiced a fairly convincing cough to make it look like I was sick and feverish. I gave my performance one more day, and then left without checking out. I'd spent the night making little "flash-bangs" out of the plastique and some pull-string detonators, as well as a couple of really sizable charges—for just in case. I went so far as to line the inside of my hat's sweat band with enough explosives to blow my head off if I were to be captured. I had that dream about Korea again when I slept that night. All three pistols were under my coat, fully loaded, with one in the chamber, when I left the hotel.

I didn't take a chance on a taxi. I walked—as carefree-appearing as anyone around me. Shop window reflections helped me stay calm. I couldn't see anyone on my tail.

Once again it was misting rain as I walked across the city towards the airport where the newspaper said the jet was sitting, under guard. I didn't really have all that far to walk. About five miles. I bought a couple of newspapers along the way, looking for any mention that it had been moved. I even stopped for an hour at a museum to check for tails, as well as window shopping so I could keep checking the storefront reflections for signs of pursuit. Nothing, at least, nothing I could see. After I left the museum, I dropped packets of plastique in random trashcans—all set to go off at the same time. It was a nice museum. I wasn't about to leave any inside. Call it an attack of morals, if you like. I don't care.

When I reached the airport, I bought a ticket for a flight east—I don't remember to where. Hungary, maybe Czechoslovakia. Wasn't important, but it used up almost all my German cash. In a restroom at the airport, I got a moment alone by loitering in a toilet until I couldn't hear anyone else in the room, then I dropped an incendiary charge into a trashcan as I dried my hands. The timer was set for half an hour. Synchronized to almost the same time I'd set for everything else. I was afraid I'd leave a trail if everything didn't go off at the same time. I wanted to divert enough of the local cops and firemen to be away from the airport, after I safely got into it.

On my way through the airport terminal, I managed to lose my coat. There was enough plastique in its pockets to make another nice little distraction. Its timers were both set to go off five minutes after the fire in the restroom. I kinda felt sorry for everyone at the airport, but I'd spread the plastique out thinly enough so that no one would be seriously injured, just scared shitless and running panicked. I really just wanted to get to the plane on the tarmac without getting shot, you know?

About the time I'd gotten to an exit that led directly out onto the airfield, I heard fire and ambulance sirens leaving towards town. I devoutly prayed that I hadn't killed anyone with my bombs back near the museum. Then the airport's fire alarms went off. My former presence in the bathroom had activated. It was time for another brief performance.

I knew that the bombs in my coat would only be five minutes behind, so I dashed for the doors. A soldier even held the door for me when I shouted *'Brand! Feuer! Das Gebäude brennt!"*

He released the door after I got out and then heroically ran deeper into the building towards the little blaze I had caused. Knowing I had, at the most, three minutes before my other little surprise packages exploded, I took off my hat and pulled the pin on the detonator inside. Tossing it at the closed door I'd just exited, I ran like a frightened rabbit towards the American jet plane I could see in the near distance. I unfastened the clasp of my briefcase as I ran.

I could see the airplane clearly now. I even recognized it. *"Oh hell,"* I said. "It's a Starfighter. I'm gonna *die.*"

Then I noticed that someone was shooting at me. Sparks leapt off the tarmac as bullets hit the gravel. I looked around quickly as I pulled the little Russian pistol and squeezed off a few rounds in their general direction, once I knew where they were, I mean.

I grabbed a bomb out of my briefcase after I'd emptied the Russian pistol, pulled the improvised detonator string with my teeth as I tossed the empty gun to the ground, I lobbed it in the general direction of the Russian guards who were shooting at me. How did I know they were Russian instead of Germans? They wore Russian uniforms. Four other, small improvised grenades followed the first as I ran towards the jet.

"The cockpit is open!" I shouted as I ran. I tossed the rest of my little home-made grenades as far as I could towards everyone who was shooting at me.

"God help me if it hasn't been fueled! I haven't got time for this!"

I pulled and emptied the other two pistols as I ran. I threw them down as soon as they were empty. I was almost there!

When I reached the plane I scrambled up the ladder as if a flight of angry hornets were right behind me. I pulled the cords on my improvised detonators on the last three large bombs I'd made, tossed them as far away as I could, then threw the ladder off the side of the plane, slammed the cockpit closed, and fired that mother up.

"Full tanks!" I rejoiced as the instrument panel came alive. I shoved the throttle home and prayed I wouldn't stall the engine out as it warmed up. It slowly began to taxi down the runway and I heard the first explosion of my homemade bombs going off. There was smoke and confusion behind me and an open runway in front of me. Agonizingly slowly, the damned Widowmaker built up speed as it crawled along the runway. I must have had all of 20 feet of runway left before that monster got up to speed. I pulled the stick back and let it climb for all it was worth. At 1500 MPH the bugger climbed as far as it could go. That took a minute and 12 seconds. At 50,000 feet I leveled out and headed West. Damn thing was shaking like Granny's old washing machine. My teeth were rattling.

I got all the systems online and checked for any kind of pursuit. I didn't like the readouts. I'd redlined everything and it hadn't had enough warm-up time. But nothing was on the radar for at least ten minutes worth of distance.

That was about the time the first air-to-air missile detonated off my left side.

"Oooooo! That was *not* polite!" I said as I pulled hard on the stick to go further towards the left—expecting my attacker to be trying to herd me into an easy target position on my right. I put the nose into a dive as I just barely sensed the explosion of the second missile on my right. But I had played this game in Korea. I dropped down like an express elevator and then faked to the right and left just barely above the treetops of some forest in West Germany at Mach 2—or as close as this particular Widowmaker could get. I vaguely heard other explosions behind me as my attacker, or attackers, totally failed to guess what I was going to do next. I was burning fuel as if it were prayer candles, or incense. If I were at altitude and a simple cruising speed, I might have been able to make 1500 miles on the amount of fuel I had at take-off. With these evasive maneuvers, I'd be lucky to get 700 miles.

And that's about the time I checked the readouts for the weapons systems. That didn't take long. There weren't any. Oh, the systems were *there*, but nothing had been loaded while the Widowmaker had been sitting as a captive at that airport in Berlin.

"OK, either I fly my way out of this, or this is gonna be a *real* short ride," I said. Along with a colorful collection of words my Granny would have whooped me for knowing.

Right about that time I saw a missile climb above me, from where I was headed! I must have been well over France by then.

"I believe the Cavalry has arrived, Tonto," I said to the shuddering and overheating piece of crap this plane was. My teeth were still rattling from the shaking it was giving me, and I hoped that I would be able to convince the bugger to fully unfold its landing gear when I had a chance to set down. More missiles launched from planes I couldn't see even on the radar because of the gyrations of this murderous, jinxy jet. Suddenly, Paris was in front of me and everything behind me became less important than getting this hunk of junk back on the ground in one piece. I pulled the throttle back, aimed at the nearest long runway, and hoped the air traffic controllers could hear me when I asked for emergency landing clearance. The radio died. Kaput. I lined the Widowmaker up on the first long runway I could see and flipped the switch for the landing gear.

I guess I'd earned at least one more miracle. I managed to land it safely.

No more damn Spooks, I thought as the jet rolled to a stop on the runway.

Of course, I was wrong. Those buggers weren't finished with me yet. The Cold War went on for *decades.*

Performance Anxiety

"Why do I always get missions that tend to blow up in my face?"— Tom Darby.

Jamaica was *supposed* to be a cakewalk...

My head snapped back as the other guy got in a punch I never saw coming. He came out of nowhere, as I was walking to a pick-up point to retrieve some papers from a dead-drop. One minute I'm wondering where I should go for lunch after I delivered the papers—the next minute some Russian agent was trying to cave in my skull.

I rolled with the punch and let my training take over. A quick kick to his solar plexus with my pointy, steel-toed cowboy boots as I leaned back from the smack in my face, and he slowed just enough for me to pop the knife in my sleeve spring into my left hand. He wheezed and leaned forward for the barest instant. I planted every inch of my Fairbairn–Sykes through his right eyeball--seven inches deep into his head. Not exactly Marquess of Queensberry rules, but I wanted to live another day and anyone who attacks me out of the blue is only asking for me to take the gloves off and fight dirty. I'm a spy, so I figure anyone who tries to kill me on a street is also a spy, but for the bad guys. Anyway, it happened right at the mouth of an alley, so I half-pushed and half-dragged his still quivering corpse ahead of me into its shadows. While his sphincters were relaxing to allow him to piss and shit himself one very final time, I searched his pockets. Left-handed shoulder holster on his right pectoral yielded a little Makarov pea-shooter. A wallet in his left inside suit coat pocket gifted me with a couple of hundred US bucks worth of Jamaican paper money. No hotel room key on him. Some kind of good luck charm on a chain around his neck. I rolled him over to search his back pockets. Nothing in his pants pockets, but an ankle holster on his right leg held a scrimshawed-ivory handled straight razor. The decoration was of a stag with huge antlers.

He'd finally died by that point, so I rolled him over on his back and pulled my knife out of his head. I used his tie to wipe his blood off of it once I'd taken a good look at his face. Rechecking his belt revealed an ammo pouch with two extra magazines for the Makarov. I took everything except for the holsters, stashed it all in a pouch on the back of my belt, under my suit coat, and left the alley by the far end from where I'd entered. I sauntered on towards the café where I was supposed to pick up the papers, had a cup of very strong coffee and pretended to read the front page of the newspaper the other papers were supposed to be inside. After some casual observation revealed no other obvious tailsI left, taking the newspaper and, I hoped, the other papers, with me. When I reached the dead-drop where I was supposed to leave the target paperwork, I saw my contact headed my way. I passed him my newspaper, he passed me his, and we separated. For the rest of the day I played tourist, but I kept an eye out for tails. Once it started getting dark, I went to a bar where I was supposed to meet another contact and make my report. I spotted her at the bar, sat on a stool next to her, and pretended to chat her up. We moved to a booth after getting our second drinks.

"You've been in a fight," she said as we eased into the booth. "There is a bruise on your jaw."

"I got intercepted," I replied. "Nothing but a little Russian pocket pistol for a clue, but obviously, I've been made. Someone knows why I'm here—or suspects why, but they know I'm an agent. You're going to have to watch your ass when you go back to the safe house. I'll hang around in plain sight for a couple of days and see if anything develops. In the meantime, nobody on the crew better make contact with me or they'll be in danger too. I delivered the papers, right on schedule, though. Now, finish your drink and slap me. Right on the bruise, if you don't mind."

"I understand," she said. Then she threw the rest of her drink in my face and smacked me harder than any woman ever had before. She stood up, all dignified and insulted, and stormed out into the gathering darkness. She was cussing me out in Portuguese, if I were to make a guess, as she stomped out of the bar. *Smart girl*, I thought as I watched her dramatic exit. *Workin' that hip-swing, too. If I live through this, I might oughta look her up once we're both back home. Could be a fun time. IF I live through this. Hell, if we BOTH live through this.*

I ordered another drink and cleaned myself up with a towel the waiter brought. Then I left and slipped into the shadows—looking for anyone who might be following me the whole time. When I finally got back to my hotel, I set up some trip-wire alarms and sat up half the night, my Colt in my right hand and the captured Makarov in my left. When dawn came, I packed my bag and checked out. I went across town and checked into another hotel I'd picked at random. Best I could tell, I wasn't being followed. I left and dropped a message at the back-up dead-drop point so the crew could find me if necessary. I also warned them that I'd been attacked, so they should treat me as if I had the plague and stay away. Then I went back to the routine I'd established as my cover—an

American businessman, import/export in trade goods and sundries. I met my business contacts, signed a few contracts, then went out for a few drinks with my clients. After that, I went back to my new hotel and got some sleep.

I followed that routine for three days. No tails that I could see, no interest in me at all as far as I could detect. I set the alarms in my room every night. Nothing ever happened.

On what I *thought* was the fourth day I woke up from a drugged stupor, handcuffed, in a hard, wooden chair in a warehouse office somewhere really quiet. My mouth tasted like a dirty bath towel had been stuffed into it. I was dehydrated, dizzy, hungover, with my head pounding and my dried sweat smelling like I'd been three days in blistering heat without a bath. *OK,* I thought. *This is either progress or a really bad thing.*

I could feel my shoulder holster was empty, and the knife's sleeve spring wasn't strapped to my arm any more. The handcuffs were tight, I was starving hungry, and I could tell from the state of my trouser legs that I'd been dragged through some filthy place while I slept. Rubbing my chin against my shirt, I could feel at least two days of beard stubble on my chin. My suit coat was missing. So were my boots. My shirt sleeve was ripped open so whoever it was could remove the sleeve spring rig from my left arm. I couldn't feel any weight from my belt pouch at the small of my back, so I guessed that it was gone as well. I don't know where that little Russian pop-gun went—I couldn't feel its miniscule weight in any of my pockets. The chair creaked from age as I wiggled about, taking inventory of what I no longer had.

I'm gonna miss those boots, I thought. *That just pisses me off. Those things cost me $80! OK, Take stock… What can I work with here? How am I going to get out of this? And what the holy hell is THIS, really? Right, two-year-old calendar on the wall, dust on the floor, dust everywhere, really. This chair sounds like it's 30 years old—I can feel it give a bit when I move and it sounds like Aunt Tilly's porch rocker with all the creaks and groans. I'm NOT tied to the chair, but I am wearing handcuffs to keep my arms behind my back. The desk in front of me looks like no one has used it for at least a year. Oh! Letter opener next to the blotter! No edge, but it has a point. Big glass paperweight next to the letter opener. OK, three weapons visible. The chair I'm in, the letter opener, and the paperweight. Now, possible impediments? Right. Whoever was bright enough to gas me in my hotel room without setting off any of the tripwires I used inside the room is not going to be stupid. They're not going to come here alone, so I'll probably have more than one assailant. I know from my training that it'll take me at least 58 seconds to get out of this chair and contort my body enough to get my hands and the handcuffs in front of me instead of behind my back. I don't have a handcuff key. I've been their captive for at least two days, maybe three, from the stink of my sweat and how much my beard has grown. Everyone else on the mission should have evacuated yesterday, if not earlier when I went missing—so, no back-up. Thanks to compartmentalization I don't know squat about why we were here or what the mission objectives were. When my interrogation starts, my choices are to play dumb—which will be easy since I don't know anything about the mission except for my little part of it. Or, I can make shit up and string the bastards along for as long as I can manage, hoping they make a fatal mistake…*

Chances of survival, slim to none. I either act like a frightened rabbit or a swaggering asshole. Or could I actually pull off acting like a swaggering asshole who IS a frightened rabbit? That might give me a couple of minutes at the right time. If they think I'm an idiot, I might have a few seconds to try and escape. OK, they captured me, and kept me unconscious for a couple of days. So, if they have an ego, they'll think I'm an idiot.

So how would a Russian think if they were in my shoes right now? Or, lack of shoes, actually… A Russian would expect physical torture, not psychological torture—or their idea of psychological torture would be way different from mine. Now, what would an ego-driven Russian think was subtle psychological torture? Oh yeah. They'll send in a hooker with a plate of food and some booze. If they know that I'm American, and why else would they trap me if they weren't sure I'm an American, they'll expect me to be starved for sex, food, and booze. God help us if they ever actually figure out our culture…

I heard a door open behind me, followed by very light footsteps accentuated by the clack-clack-clack of a woman wearing high heels. A moment later, a pretty, dark-haired girl of about 20, wearing a short, tight dress, fishnet stockings, and possessing a spectacular figure appeared— carrying a tray of food in both hands, with a six-pack of PBR in one hand, under the tray. Her dress was dark blue, short, and had a reasonably plunging neckline. By the time she had placed the tray and the beer on the desk, she'd made it obvious that there was nothing under her dress except for her lightly-tanned skin. She made a show of cleaning the dust away from the desk. I could smell steak cooked medium rare, a baked potato, and mushrooms in a brown gravy as well as her apricot perfume. I could see a small slab of butter, as well as one of those tiny loaves of French bread on the tray, too.

I heard a guard, or someone, close the door as she dusted off the desk to make it clean enough to serve as a table. *She's not alone, then,* I thought. *As I expected, she has watchers.*

"I have been instructed to see that you eat, and to make you—comfortable," she said. The pause was enough to tell me just exactly what level of "comfort" she was being made to supply. Her English sounded as if her language tutor had been French. Nice voice, though, not too low-pitched, just perfect for a woman five foot six or so—as she was. Not a pretend voice.

"*Spasibo, no ya, kazhetsya, neskol'ko s ogranichennymi vozmozhnostyami.*" I've never been all that good at Russian, but I thought it best to appear to be polite. I shrugged as I rattled my handcuffs a little bit. Saying thank you, but indicating that the handcuffs were a bit of a handicap to eating a meal—or any other activity, seemed to be just good manners on my part.

"I can unlock your restraints," she said. "But if you attempt to escape, we will *both* face—consequences."

"Thank you," I replied, mostly abandoning my pitiable attempts to speak Russian. "On my honor as an Officer and a Gentleman, I will do nothing to place you at risk. I find myself both thirsty and hungry. But the tray you brought holds only enough for one hungry man. Am I expected to be so *nekulturny* as to dine while you partake of nothing? I refuse to be forced to be—uncultured. Is it permissible for my captors to allow you to join me at dinner? I would far prefer such a beautiful woman as yourself to be my dinner companion, rather than to see you relegated to the role of a servant." I gave her, and whoever was watching whatever cameras were undoubtedly spying on me, my best Southern Charm smile.

She paled, her flawless skin turning white as if in shock. Obviously, I had gone off-script. Good. The more they thought I was just trying to play the gentleman in pursuit of a later seduction, the more they would underestimate me later on.

"I am not sure if that will be permitted—" she began, only to be interrupted by a knock at the door and the entry of a burly guard in a uniform I didn't recognize, carrying a second tray of food, as well as a bottle of wine and two wine glasses. *Check,* I thought. *I was anticipated. They're good. That'll make my escape even harder.*

The erstwhile "waiter" sat the second tray and the wine bottle and glasses on the desk next to the tray and beer meant for me, then exited as wordlessly as he had entered."*Ty moya blagodarnost,*" I said to his retreating back. The clack of the door's lock being refastened echoed through the room.

"*Dolzhny li my poobedat', Moya Ledi?*" I asked my companion. Without another word, she moved to stand behind me and unfasten my handcuffs.

"Your Russian is—somewhat unusual," she said. I stood and flexed my cramped muscles, smiled, then moved to take my indicated seat at the desk.

"As if I learned it from a book, instead of hearing someone actually say the words?" I asked. "For that is true. I did learn from books, but many words I have never heard spoken before. I beg your forgiveness for my ignorance. To put the shoe on the other foot, as we say in the US, you sound as if your tutor for English was French. Nothing wrong with that. Your accent makes you sound very—intriguing."

"Thank you," she said. "Shall we dine?"

"Would that we had a proper table," I said as she sat in the desk chair and I sat opposite in the creaky chair I'd woken up in.

"People in our business often have to improvise when the need arises," she replied. "Wine or beer?"

"I think perhaps beer for now," I said. "I need the water. I'm quite parched from your knockout gas."

"You have our apologies," she said as she handed me a can of beer and some silverware wrapped in a cloth napkin. "We were in somewhat of a rush to extricate you from your hotel before any harm befell you. Might I compliment you on the excellence of your defensive measures? You set us a pretty puzzle as to how we could overcome them."

"I do my best with what I have to work with," I said as I put butter on my potato and began to cut my steak. "If you don't mind me asking," I said as I took a bite of the steak. "Oh, excellent," I added as soon as I had swallowed, "I'd like to know why I am here, and not in some torture cell."

"You would have been," she said. "If not for our intervention. Your enemies were somewhat difficult to dissuade when we intercepted them at your hotel room door. You might be relieved to know that they are in custody—those who survived our arrival. The Courts in Geneva will most likely trade them for others of our own captured agents, if at all possible. The—casualties—were removed quietly, afterward."

"Sorry I missed the action," I said. "Or perhaps I shouldn't be." I ate some more of the excellent meal and opened a second beer. "But you make it sound as if," I added between bites. "As if you rescued me rather than being my captors. I am not sure that I understand your part in this little ballet. You aren't part of the Russian team who tried to kill me earlier?"

"You may find this difficult to believe," she said as she took another bite of the Chicken Parmesan on her own plate. After a small sip of her wine, she continued. "I hold no love for the East Germans, or their Russian masters. I was born in a quiet part of Poland, but I live and work in Switzerland now. The War was difficult for my family. I lost many to the fighting—both directly and through our resistance. I was only a child, then. Afterwards, I found myself recruited by an organization loosely affiliated with the United Nations." She tore off a bit of the French bread and slathered butter on it. I have to admit; it was good bread. I followed her example and took a bite from my own loaf. Cutting another bite of steak, I patiently waited for more of her story. I savored every morsel of my meal. Patience came easy in such a situation. Escape was going to be hard enough. Though much harder if I remained hungry and dehydrated.

"You don't look old enough for that," I said. "I took you for twenty-five or so."

"Thank you," she replied. "I am thirty-two. I was five when the war began."

"I was four, myself. We're nearly the same age," I said. "So, tell me more about this UN agency you work for."

"You Americans," she said. "You are good, and tough, and fine allies, but there are secrets being kept from you. The English are particularly adept at keeping secrets from you. Tell me honestly, has anyone ever told you anything at all about a tall blue box?"

"Not a word," I answered. "Though I'm not much more than a glorified airplane pilot, so I wouldn't expect to be in the inner circle for any secrets. I'm only groundside because I have a few useful skills the spooks needed down here."

"I thought as much. What I am about to tell you is highly classified," she said.

I took the last bite of my steak, followed swiftly by the last of the mushrooms and baked potato, then buttered the final bit of my bread, sat it down, and opened a third beer while I waited for her to continue. "I'm all ears," I said as I savored the last of my bread loaf.

"Would it surprise you," she said. "To be told that our world is facing threats which make this 'Cold War' look as if it were a mere kindergarten sandbox squabble?"

"Lady," I answered. "After Korea, everything looks like a schoolyard dust-up to me. Please go on. You interest me, strangely."

"Please call me Anna," she said. "Anna Woźniak. The organization I work for has been chartered to protect us, you and I and everyone—even the Russians—from a larger threat. From many larger threats, in fact." She sipped the last of her wine and sat her empty plate aside, as I did myself a few moments earlier. I finished the rest of my can of beer as she gathered her thoughts to continue. "Some years ago," she finally said. "A stranger appeared in London, England. He 'assisted' the British Army with some—rather strange matter involving their Underground railways. By the time the affair had concluded, higher ups had discerned the need for a permanent team, or rather, several teams, of rather *Special* Forces. I was recruited due to my childhood experiences as part of the Polish Resistance to the Nazis during the last World War. As I said, I am based in Switzerland now—as part of one of those Special Forces. We rescued you here and now, in the hope of recruiting you into our organization as well. This would not, should not, ever cause a conflict with your duties as an American soldier—"

"Airman," I gently corrected her. "And part-time spy."

"Just so," she replied. "You would be a consultant. Not assigned to any particular group, serving alongside fellow Americans, and British, and whosoever else your Team Leader feels would be of use in any given situation. If you accept, we will return you to your 'spooks' as you call them, but with the understanding that they would release you if and when duty to our group requires. This would entail a slight bonus to your normal pay packet, with other bonuses if we need you, and otherwise, a bit of special training to bring you up to speed with our units. If you refuse this offer, we will return you to your employers unharmed. This, I give you my word, either way, you will be free to go home, unmolested."

"How long do I have to decide?" I asked.

"Until dawn," Anna replied. "Likely, we will never meet again, in any case. However, dawn is many hours away. I am of a mind to make the most of the time we have together."

She stood and reached behind her back. I could hear the zipper of her dress sliding down.

"Are you sure about this, Anna?" I asked. "I'm just a farm boy from the Southern US. I'm probably not as sophisticated as the guys in your class, like you're used to."

The zipper sound stopped, and she shrugged her shoulders out of the straps of her dress. "After surviving the Nazis as a child and the Russians ever since, and more that you wouldn't believe—I decided long ago that if I wanted someone, I would not forgo the chance. Our lives could end in an instant—poof! Gone to ashes and dust. And we might never know that our time was over before the bombs fell. Are you unwilling? Am I too forward and aggressive for you?"

"That desk looks mighty uncomfortable for what you've got in mind," I said.

"You'd be surprised," Anna replied. "But there is a *chaise longue* just over there—away from the lamp. Would that suit you?"

"Lead the way," I said as I began to unbutton my shirt. "But I warn you, I really need a shower first."

"Nonsense," she said as her dress hit the floor and she stepped out of it. "I will pretend you are French."

I learned a lot that night. But I kept an eye on the door all the same. Some training you never forget.

The next morning, the scent of strong coffee tickled my nose as I awoke. I was still "entangled" with Anna as we shared the long sofa, covered only by a thin silk sheet. I looked over at the desk and saw not only a coffee pot, but two plates loaded with what, from here, looked to be omelets, link sausages, and hash browns, and THERE WERE GRITS ON ONE OF THE PLATES! Toast and marmalade and butter between the plates on a small serving tray. I heard the room's door quietly thump shut and the clack of the lock being turned. Must have missed our waiter by mere seconds.

"Where the hell do you get grits in Jamaica?" I asked out loud. Sitting up carefully, I tried not to disturb Anna, but ultimately failed.

"Is this what all American boys are like?" she said as she awoke. "Does the arrival of breakfast distract them from any possible appetizers?"

"Southern boys are a breed apart," I answered her. "However, a dessert after breakfast is not against our upbringing."

"I shall hold you to that," she replied. "Oh, omelets! Yes, those should never be allowed to become cold! No *brioche*? Oh well, we aren't in France." She got up off of the couch as I was groping on the floor for my pants. They weren't where I'd dropped them. "Come, eat," she added as she walked to the impromptu table the desk had become—unashamed of her nakedness. "We will eat and then I will show you where the shower is—and then, perhaps that dessert you spoke of?"

Having breakfast naked, with a beautiful woman who was also naked, was a novel experience for me. However, I thereby resolved to make it another learning experience. Breakfast was wonderful, the shower was heavenly, and "dessert" was well worth waiting for. Afterwards, I found that our clothes from the day before had been freshly laundered, pressed, and were ready to be worn. Not only that, but under my clothes were all the weapons and ammo I had before I was liberated, and beside the sofa were my boots!

"Be honest with me," I said as I fastened my belt and leaned down to get the pouch with my captured weapons inside. "How much of last night was 'recruiting' and how much was spontaneous?"

"None of it was recruiting," Anna replied. "I've seen enough horrors in my time to convince me that whatever pleasures come our way should never be ignored. Postponed, perhaps, but not passed by if there is time."

"What about the rest of my team?" I asked.

"Completed their mission and went home," she replied. "While you were asleep under the influence of our tranquilizers. Your superiors have been informed of our actions—the group's actions, not ours personally. They await your decision, as do my own."

"I'm in," I replied. "Will I ever see you again?"

"Most likely not," she answered. "Hence my abandon last night. Unless circumstances bring us together again, and that is unlikely, last night was all the time we will ever have."

"OK, that's life," I said. "But I won't soon forget you."

"Or I you. Welcome to our unit," she said as she kissed me one last time.

72 hours later, I was back on the ground in California. After the gentlest debriefing I had ever had in my life, I found myself assigned some additional training under a British officer.

"Major Jones?" The soft-spoken voice of a junior officer intruded upon the aforesaid Major's morning paperwork. The accent was decidedly Southern England, proclaiming the Lieutenant was from the Portsmouth, Gosport, Southsea region.

"Yes, Alderson? Something new?" The Major's accent was Welsh, with a hint of wider influences during his lifetime.

"We have received a Moondust Alert report from the American Southwest," said the Lieutenant. "Sorry to bother you, Sir. It isn't marked 'Urgent,' yet we have been instructed to put together a team to investigate—since we are the closest detachment to the scene."

"Considering that our 'detachment' consists of yourself, myself, and a squad of soldiers," the Major replied. "I believe we would need to liaise with our hosts for additional support. Where is the site?"

"Sixty miles west of Socorro, New Mexico," the Lieutenant replied. "The report," he added as he handed Major Jones the paperwork. "The site is roughly two miles east of a town named Datil, and roughly twenty miles further south of there. Not much to be seen except for desert, cacti, tumbleweeds, and the occasional cattle ranch. The US Army has the site isolated and is keeping the local ranchers away. They've requested our participation as consultants."

"So," replied the Major as he flipped rapidly through the few pages of the report. "Something came down, and they want us to help them prevent another 'Roswell' incident?"

"From what I could discern from the report, that would be my best guess as well, Sir." The Lieutenant smiled slightly. "My guess is that it is a burned-out satellite, possibly Soviet but also possibly Chinese. Both have a minority of orbiting experiments that could possibly have fallen. If it were a US project, we wouldn't have been allowed to know about this. If it were British, it damn well wouldn't have fallen at all. That we were called in indicates that the US can't identify the debris and wants us to advise."

"And if it is none of the above, Lieutenant?"

"Well then, the agreement between the US and the UN would place us in charge of any investigation. You, as the Senior Officer on-site, would be obliged to commandeer any US resource available, up to and including a nuclear air-strike, if you deem it necessary."

"Just so," replied Major Jones. "Very well, put together a full investigative team. Requisition whatever experts can be rounded up, air transport able to reach the site, a platoon of US squaddies, and place our own boys in command of each of the US squads. Give our squad Acting ranks high enough the Americans can't gripe about having to take orders from us. Sergeant-Majors, perhaps. You know the paperwork involved much better than I."

"What about our new, local boy, Sir?"

"The pilot? Yes, good idea, Alderson. Tell him it is part of his training. Assign him as my Aide," said Major Jones. "You'll remain here to advise Geneva as to what we find, if anything. But be ready to mobilize a full response if this goes tits up."

"You believe this might be a BBB incident, sir?" The Lieutenant's question hung in the air like a bomb just released from its bomb bay.

"I believe in not leaving things to chance," replied Major Jones. "IF, and only if, this turns out to be more than it looks like from this preliminary report—I will want every option available at a moment's notice. Probably, it is just junk that fell. If it *is* something more? Well, being prepared is part of our mission."

"Understood, Sir." Lieutenant Alderson said, snapped off a salute, and left Major Jones alone with his thoughts. Jones stood, looked around his tiny, borrowed office at Edwards Air Force Base, then looked out the windows, lost in thought. Finally, he picked up the telephone on his desk and put through a call to his batman.

"Arthur," Jones said to his Personal Aide. "Pack my kit for a Moondust incident—yours as well. We have an assignment. Special equipment? The usual bagatelle, seal it in a crate marked 'Emergency Equipment' and stand ready.

I'll send you the details when I know them. Oh, desert gear, for us, primarily. You know what the Yanks have to offer us, so use your own judgement as to what extras we might need ourselves. Yes, be ready for a 'drop everything and go' situation. Alderson is off making arrangements with the Base Commander's staff. My best guess for any of the boffins the Yanks can round up for us is 8 to 24 hours before we can leave. I leave our personal preparations in your capable hands, Sergeant-Major. Pull rank if and as needed. Prod buttocks as you see fit. I'll call you again with a more accurate estimate as to when the flag goes up, just as soon as I know. This is probably nothing exciting, but one can never tell in our line of work. No, no one has heard a peep out of the bugger in years, to the best of my knowledge. But I'm on a 'need to know' footing, here. There might have been other incidents I wasn't briefed upon."

"Now, we wait," said Jones as he hung up the phone. Moodily, he stared out his office window at the American airbase.

A Corporal came by my quarters and told me to report to the Base Commander's office. So I cleaned up as fast as possible, got in uniform, and caught a jeep over to Headquarters.

"Captain Darby, reporting for duty, Sir." I said as I snapped off a salute once I was in the General's office.

"As you were, sit down, Captain. I have an assignment for you."

"Yes Sir," I replied as I sat in the proffered chair.

"You recently have accepted additional duties with a UN organization," began the General. "This is one of their missions. You have been assigned as an Aide to their local Major, Jones is his name, on the base here. You are to consider this as advanced training. Here is all I know. At 21:35 hours yesterday, debris from a fallen orbital device impacted approximately 20 miles east southeast of Datil, New Mexico. Major Jones and his team have received orders to meet up with the US forces who have cordoned off the impact area, attempt to discover the origin of the debris, assess any threat, and collect whatever evidence is salvageable at the site. They have requested three cargo helicopters and crew, a platoon of troops, and whatever scientific advisors we can round up on short notice. The soldiers will be placed under the command of Major Jones' own squad of specialists. The scientists we can get are all enroute from various locations, as we speak. Your duties are to assist Major Jones, observe, train for future incidents of this kind, and deliver a discrete report to me, personally, upon your return. Is this clear?"

"Yessir," I replied. "Major Jones and Sergeant-Major Heath have been training me already, as has Lieutenant Alderson. I have also been on a few training exercises with Sergeant Devon and his squad as well, mostly long hikes to learn some advanced wilderness survival skills, a bit of geology, and skills useful to being assigned to archeology digs."

"I am not sure this UN task force is altogether useful to the US, but orders are orders," said the General. "Still, from what I have been briefed, they could prove to be a valuable asset. Very well, do you accept the assignment?"

"Sir, yessir!" I replied. *Anything to break the monotony of being groundside when I want to be flying,* I thought to myself. "How much time do I have before H-Hour and is there any special gear I need to requisition?"

"The scientific experts should arrive within 10 hours. If you have an hour past that estimate, I would be astounded. This is a top security mission, Captain. You will perform your duties to this UN group to the best of your ability, return, and report personally to me—and me alone. Is that understood?"

"Yessir," I replied. *Anna,* I thought, *what have I gotten myself into because you thought I was good enough to join your unit?* "Train, observe, and report back to you. You can count on me, Sir. One question—do you want a written report, or just face to face?"

"That would be situational, Captain Darby," the General replied. "This UN Intelligence Taskforce seems, on the surface, to be a collection of crackpots and weirdos. But if they aren't, and they have intel that the US needs for our own security, we will need a full, formal report to file with the Pentagon. If this is just some Russian sputnik falling out of the sky, then a verbal report will do."

"Understood, Sir," I said. "If it's just normal junk that fell from orbit, then only you need to know. But if it turns out to be any of that 'flying saucer' bullshit, I'll write up a full, detailed, formal report for you."

"I didn't say anything about any damn flying saucers, Captain." The General's face went red. "There isn't going to be another damn Roswell bullshit incident on MY watch—is that clear?"

"Sir! Yes, Sir!" I replied.

"Dismissed," said the General. "Grab your gear and whatever you think you'll need for a week in the New

Mexico desert. Report to Major Jones as soon as you're ready to go. That is all, Captain."

I saluted as I got up out of the chair, turned, and left the General's office without another word.

Half an hour later I was standing in Major Jones' office, reporting for duty. My bug-out bag was at my feet. Most of the time it took me to get ready was swapping US gear for UN-spec gear. Except for my Colt, strapped to my hip as it normally was. I decided I would only leave that behind if I were given specific orders from Major Jones.

"Tom Darby, reporting for duty, Sir." I said as I saluted Major Jones. "You requested me, Sir?"

Jones returned my salute and gestured that I should stand at ease. Only a Brit can do that so effortlessly.

"Yes, your training with us has gone splendidly so far. But now we have a live exercise of what we have been training you for, so think of this as an advanced course. As of 21:35 hours last night, something impacted the ground near a village called 'Datil' in your state of New Mexico. It may be nothing. It may be a Russian Satellite, or even a Chinese satellite we were previously unaware of having been launched that has fallen to ground. It may be a worthless chunk of rock. Or it may be a threat our forces will need to deal with. We won't know until we reach the site and give the scientific experts your government is rounding up time to assess the situation. If worst comes to worst, the object will be either a known, or as yet unknown, threat. Barring that unlikely possibility, our purview is to secure the site, let the scientists examine the debris and file reports as to whatever they find--as well as our own impressions. I expect this to be something innocuous. However, my assignment is to be prepared in case it is not. Do you understand, Captain?"

"Yes sir," I replied. "It's probably nothing. It might be something the Commies put in orbit. Or it might be something dangerous. I'm ready, sir. I packed everything I could think of that might be useful in case 'dangerous' is the final determination. As well as extra C-Rations and water, desert survival gear, some gadgets my Spook friends gave me, and anything I could think of that my dad and grandfather recommended to take if I were headed into an unknown situation."

"Oh?" said the Major. "Forgive my curiosity, but just what would that be?"

"A Gurkha knife my Dad was given by a Nepalese soldier during his time in the Philippines. It was a gift between battlefield survivors. Dad said it was better than any machete ever issued by the US Army. 100 yards of quarter-inch rope—Granddaddy always said a kit without rope was an unfinished kit. A pocket magnifying glass to start fires without matches during the daytime. A ball of twine and half a dozen brass bells—to use as a tripwire alarm around a campsite. A Swiss Army pocket knife to use as a multi-functional tool, a small single-edge hatchet with a hammer back-face and an assortment of nails and whatnot to use in setting up a campsite. A clay sculptor's cutting wire tool with hand grips on both ends—Daddy killed a Nazi guard with it during the D-Day liberation of France. I swapped out my M1 rifle for a short-barrel, folding stock Beretta M59 chambered for .308 NATO— and packed 300 rounds for it. Three 20-round magazines and 12 stripper clips to save space. An ammo belt with 120 rounds for my Colt, pre-loaded in magazines. With another 200 rounds in the box, stored in a belt pouch. A pair of wire-cutters. A dozen flash-bangs courtesy of the CIA, as well as a few smoke grenades. C-Rations for four weeks. Three canteens of water—good for 36 hours of starvation rationing for one man, in a pinch. And some basic campground cooking gear that the US Army issues to troops. A pup tent, tent stakes, and rope for that, too."

"You could teach survival classes to our troops," said Major Jones, obviously impressed.

"There was a lot of stuff that would have come in handy in a forest or near a river that I took out of my kit, sir," I replied. "New Mexico is fresh out of forests and there are damn few lakes or rivers. I thought it prudent to customize my kit to the situation at hand, as best I knew it. I was raised in the Appalachians, the mountain range near the US East Coast. My family survived anything that got thrown at them since the US became a country. If my family had a motto, it'd be 'improvise, adapt, and prepare.' We tend to do well in survival courses. My original training Sergeant and I were both docked 5 points for gaining three pounds each on my wilderness survival test. I unraveled one of my spare socks and used a bent safety pin as a fish hook and grubs from a fallen log as bait. We were eating fresh bream and the occasional rabbit while my fellow platoon members were eating the grubs and worms like I was using for fish-bait. We snared rabbits using the cheese from our C-Rations as bait and a snare made from our boot laces and a bent tree branch as a trap. But Sarge and I still got the highest score for the exercise...."

"I am impressed," said the Major. "I have asked that you be assigned to me as my Aide during this mission. Of course, you will still be subordinate to Sergeant-Major Beckett, of my personal staff. Lieutenant Alderson will remain on base to mind the store, so to speak. We will leave as soon as the scientists all arrive. Something under 12 hours from now. Sorry I can't be more specific, But I have to depend on your superiors to round up the necessary boffins and herd them to the base."

"I fully understand, Sir," I replied. "I will be in my quarters. Give me five minutes notice to hijack a jeep and I'll be on the airfield when we are ready to leave. You have my telephone extension."

"Yes, dismissed, Captain," said Major Jones.

48 hours later, the three US helicopters landed 30 miles south southeast of Datil, New Mexico. The site was a debris field, roughly a quarter mile wide and three times that in length. Major Jones and his men exited the aircraft and took their first good look around. Issuing orders to the US troops already present, the Major started the collection of evidence from the far edges of the crash. Everyone bagged up whatever their searches revealed. Metallic trash lightly littered the ground close to the helicopter landing site, becoming more concentrated as one approached the site's eastern border. It wasn't until the unit group neared the last 50 yards of the crash site that any debris larger than an automobile license plate was visible.

"That's not right," said Major Jones. He pointed towards a piece of metal about the size of the door of a kitchen oven. "The lettering is Cyrillic, as Russian ought to be, but they misspelled Sputnik—there is an extra letter. And that says that it is part of *'Sputnick 21.'* Sputnik doesn't have a C in it—in Russian or English, and the Russians renamed their satellites long before a '21' in the Sputnik series would have been launched. Someone is trying to fake being Russian. And there is something off with the grammar. This reads like it was written by a Chinese person pretending to be Russian. Or by someone pretending to be Chinese, pretending to be Russian. And they didn't do their research very well."

"You mean it's a *fake* Russian satellite?" I asked.

"Considering that we have no reports of China as even close to being able to launch anything more than short-range missiles," the Major replied. "I'd say someone is playing silly buggers, yes."

"And they've lost some of the pieces," said the Major's personal aide.

"Sergeant-Major?" I asked. "What--"

"It was a joke, son," Sergeant-Major Beckett replied.

"Major? I don't see anything other than this piece that is larger than a paperback book," Tom said. "Not in all this debris. And none of that stuff seems to be as heavily-built as this bit with the lettering. Is it possible that this was meant to survive the crash—to give us a false clue?"

"Bit of a red herring, eh?" the Major replied. "Good point, lad. Arthur, my compliments to Sergeant-Major Heath and inform him to spread Devon and our men out with the US detachment and the scientists. Let's finish collecting all this scrap and get it back to base where it can be studied properly. I want each one of our lads to take photos of every concentration of debris they find before anyone picks anything up. We don't have time to do any proper 'archeology' today. But I want a photographic record, nonetheless."

"Very good Sir, however, I anticipated your orders and have already instructed our boys to do exactly that. I'll just go and see that no one is slacking." Beckett replied. "Lad," he said to me. "You stick with the Major and ask him all the questions you can think of—you Yanks excel at that."

"Thank you, sir—I think." I said.

"Now, why do you suppose someone would want us to think that they were Russians," asked the Major when we were alone. "Or for that matter, Chinese pretending to be Russian?"

"Protective coloration?" I replied. "Someone is trying to blend in and hide. The question on my mind is are we supposed to believe that they're Russian, or believe that they're Chinese pretending to be Russian, or is this someone expecting us to see through that and start worrying about who *else* could pull off an undetected satellite launch—and what the hell else have they got planned?"

"That is some genius-level paranoia you have there," said the Major as he laughed. "You have been working with those CIA lads for quite a while. Methinks their mind-set is beginning to rub off on you."

"I never minded it back when I was just flying and taking pictures for them," I said. "But working with them on the ground? That'll drive you crazy."

"Understood. And I agree with you," said the Major. "To an extent. However, there is a far deeper level of secrets than even *they* are privy to—and that's where *we* come in. You don't have the clearance for me to tell you about that. Not just yet. I can't even begin to tell you just how deep this particular rabbit hole goes—not today.

You're a smart lad. I can see why you were assigned to us. But if and when you do get the necessary clearance? Well, I could tell you stories that would make your hair curl."

"Curiouser and curiouser," I replied.

"Just so," said Major Jones.

"Oh dear," I said. "If we're *supposed* to see that this is a third party pretending to be someone else—what are they playing at? What're their goals? What do they hope to trick us into thinking?"

"Welcome to a larger world, my boy," replied the Major. "Welcome to a larger world. If you really want the answers to those questions, I can expedite your clearance levels being raised. But that would entail you being permanently seconded to our little UN group. Normally, you would carry out your duties as a US Armed Forces member, but if we needed you, for something like this little jaunt—or something more serious, your superiors would send you wherever *we* needed you, for however long we needed you, and you would be under the command of one or more of our officers for the duration of that mission. And I can promise you, our missions are either a little cakewalk like this, or deadly danger. There isn't usually an in-between. Life expectancy on our more serious missions is measured in minutes, or hours—or decades. Not much middle ground to be had there."

"I was a combat pilot in Korea before I was old enough to buy a beer here in the US, Sir. The threat of sudden death isn't something I'm unacquainted with," I replied. "I will consider everything carefully, Sir. But for now, I'm in. It's not like working for the spooks has a guaranteed happy ending and retirement plan."

"No rush," said the Major. "I will file the paperwork if you agree, but not until you do so. Are we clear on that?"

"Yes, Sir!" I replied. "I will think it over very carefully." But I already knew what my answer would be. If there was a bigger picture to be seen—over and above what I already knew—I couldn't let that opportunity pass. Curiosity killed the cat, they say. But cats have nine lives. So satisfaction brings them back. Little did I know… Looking back on it now, I probably would have been safer with the spooks. At least a spy can only die once.

Shore Leave

"Even vacations got interesting, sometimes…"
— Tom Darby.

I had the road all to myself, until some local cop got a hard-on…

I'd taken my bonus money and bought myself a Harley. A 1968 1200 cc Panhead Electra Glide, with one of those new electric starters. It was great for on base, and kept me from having to hijack a jeep to get around. Lots of pilots buy motorcycles. It's the only road vehicle that feels like a fighter jet, you know? So when I got some leave time and decided to head for Daytona, I was eager to have myself a nice long road trip. All I wanted was a road, some cold beer, to see the sun rise over the ocean, and maybe find a companionable lady for some pleasant bar-hopping times once I got there. The siren behind me was a bit of a surprise. First there was no cop, then there was a cop. Fellow must have been sitting off one of the side roads I'd passed.

When I left the base in California, I headed for Meteor Crater in Arizona for the day—just sight-seeing, then on to Socorro, New Mexico for a night, then south a bit towards Dallas, Texas. Just stopped for gas and some food there at a truck stop. From there I rolled on across the Mississippi River, and further south to New Orleans. Had a quiet weekend there at a motor lodge outside the city limits. Nice local bar and a restaurant that had some good Cajun cooking, close by the motel. Then I went on towards Florida. Dead reckoning told me I was somewhere in South Alabama, and that's where things started to go to shit.

I pulled off the road and shut the bike down, then grabbed my license and military ID from my leather jacket pocket. *I could have just gone to Long Beach…* I thought. *But NO, I wanted to see the sun rise over the Atlantic…*

The fat walrus that got out of the cop car couldn't have been long out of High School. He unsnapped the strap on the holster for his .38 as he swaggered towards me. *Great,* I thought. *Schoolyard bully. I bet he has a Klan robe in the trunk of the patrol car. If he calls me Boy…*

"You in a heap of trouble, Boy" he said as he got within talking range. "We don't allow motor-sickles in this county." His hand never left the butt of his pistol as he got closer.

"Captain," I replied. "US Air Force. Captain Tom Darby. Not *Boy…* I'm an officer and a gentleman, or so says the US Congress. Is there a problem, officer?"

Teach would have taken this little boy's gun away and shoved it where the sun don't shine, by now. But I'm not Teach. I decided to act offended, but polite. Better than gettin' shot by a moron, anyway.

My .45 and its kit was in my saddlebags. Might as well be on the moon for all the good it would be in there. I had my derringer in the breast pocket of my leather jacket, but drawing down on a policeman wasn't an option at the moment. My options were very few at the moment. I was either gonna get shot, or try and sucker this guy close enough for me to punch him into the middle of next week.

Sirens split the air. A Fury and a T-Bird screeched up between me and the cop. Four guys got out of the Fury, two got out of the Thunderbird. The driver of the T-Bird got out with a .44 magnum revolver pointed at the cop. "FBI," he said. "Stand down right now or I *will* give you a vasectomy with this hand-cannon. I promise, you'll be speaking in a voice only dogs can hear for at least three weeks. Take your hand off your pistol and go up to the hood of your patrol car. Assume the position. Boys, make sure he complies."

I knew that voice. When he turned to look at me, I was sure. It was Joe, my TO from Korea. What have I just walked into?

The cop blustered for about half a second, then put his hands up. Joe looked at his crew, then said "Make it a three-day hospital stay," then turned to face me as the other five guys began to beat the living hell out of the cop. Joe put his pistol away, walked up to me, grinned, and said "I've got something I need for you to do, Tom."

I tried to ignore the sounds of the cop getting his ass handed to him.

"Is that really necessary?' I asked, nodding my head towards the cop getting beaten down.

"No, but he won't ever play asshole with anyone ever again," Joe replied. "Sometimes you have to put these Crackers in their place."

"Seems a bit extreme," I said.

"I'll call an ambulance when we leave," Joe said. "He'll live. My boys are trained to be careful. But I need you to do something for me."

"So you said," I replied as I turned my back to the fight. "What? And thank you for showing up when you did."

"Walk with me," Joe said as he led me away from the crime scene. We ambled a few yards up the highway. "You're welcome," he added when we were about twenty feet away from the cars. "There's a sub off the coast of Florida," he added. "Maybe Russian, maybe Chinese, I need you to find out who they are and why they're there and what they're interested in."

"And how am I supposed to do that?" I asked. I heard car doors slam behind me. Evidently Joe's guys were finished with their 'assignment.' "Sneak onboard a sub at sea? I don't have the slightest idea how I can do that."

Joe turned around and headed back to the Thunderbird. Naturally, I followed. "I hear you have connections, nowadays. You'll improvise something." He got behind the wheel of the T-Bird and picked up a radio mike. "You need to leave. Now," he added as he switched the radio to the police band frequency he wanted. "Officer down, need assistance…" he added as he spoke into the radio. He gave our location along Highway 10. "Just go on to Daytona," he said to me as he hung the mike back up. "Like you were planning to do. Then ask your friends for some help. This is important. They have resources we don't. But be careful. I don't want anything to happen to you." Joe slammed the car door, backed up, turned around, and peeled off down the highway back the way he'd come. The Fury followed close behind.

I looked at the cop, bleeding on the road, got back on my bike and cranked it up. "Couldn't happen to a nicer guy," I said as I kicked the bike in gear and took off Eastward.

I still wonder if I meant the cop, or me…

Fourteen hours later I was pulling into Daytona. Still hadn't decided.

I made a few phone calls once I checked into my motel. My English unit told me that someone would meet me, gave me an estimated time, and recommended that I go to a certain restaurant. It wasn't exactly a dive, but I decided that it had seen better days, once I arrived. The shrimp and seafood platter were delicious though. I sipped my second beer and waited. Eventually, a blonde slid into the booth seat opposite me and leaned in close to talk. Never seen her before, and I was about to tell her that I didn't need any "company" right then, but she dropped Major Jones' name. Suddenly, I was all ears.

"Your friends were correct," she said, just barely loud enough for me to hear above the music the band was playing off in a corner of the room. "There is something there. It seems to be something quite large."

Her British accent tickled my ears pleasantly. She was a looker, too. Short skirt, floaty blouse, nice tan. Smelled like apricots. "Go on," I said. I leaned in closer so that she could talk more quietly. Her smile was even nicer.

"Major Jones said to tell you that the sub is fifty miles off-shore. From the size, it doesn't appear to be Chinese. But it doesn't match any Russian submarines we have on record, either."

The way she pronounced 'either' as if it started with an I, pegged her as English. "Any targets in the area?" I asked.

"It is close enough to observe any test flights from your Canaveral Space Center," she said. "But here is nothing on their official schedule. However, there are reports of an unscheduled nuclear weapons platform launch that our mutual friends are somewhat concerned over. If that sub were to have electronic jamming capabilities, it could possibly interfere with that launch."

"That would be a bad thing," I said.

"Only if you think a plethora of orbital nuclear weapons are a good thing," she said. She sighed. "Aren't the bombs and rockets enough?"

"Not my circus, not my monkeys," I replied. "I'm no expert. I just fly planes. Still, derailing a nuke meant to go into orbit might just ruin everyone's day."

"Half a dozen 'nukes,' all on one orbital platform? That could indeed become a problem. And this is just the first of possibly dozens more orbital weapons platforms. Several dozen, if our Soviet and Chinese playmates follow suit."

I raised my glass in acknowledgement of her point. "Make that launch fall on Miami or Cuba and go boom? Yeah, that'd be a bad thing for the whole world. We're close enough to World War Three as it is…"

"Indeed," she replied. "Order me a drink. If I don't act as if I were a date you were expecting, I might look like a prostitute. That could have—repercussions, later."

"What'll you have?" I asked, while signaling to a waiter.

"Beer," she said. "If I order a gin and tonic it will interfere with my cover as an American business secretary."

Her American accent when the waiter took her order sounded nothing like her normal speaking voice. I was impressed. She sounded like girls I had met in Knoxville or Atlanta. If I didn't already know better, I'd swear she was native-born. Once her beer and a clean plate so she could share my meal arrived, she gave the waiter enough time to walk out of earshot before she continued. I offered her some of the shrimp and stuffed crab from my seafood platter. She ate daintily, like a cat.

"Thank you," she said.

"You have English table manners, I see. Might want to watch that—if your cover is a girl from Georgia," I said.

"I'll have to work on that," she replied. "Some habits *are* rather ingrained, I fear. You may have just prevented me from blowing my cover. If not today, then in the future. Thank you, again."

"Think nothing of it. Professional courtesy. OK, how am I supposed to get fifty miles out to a sub that's hiding underwater? And what do I do when I get there?"

"It just so happens that there is an oceanography expedition headed that way tomorrow," she said. "Officially, they are going to be filming for one of those television specials that are so popular these days. They have a rather brightly-painted and *highly*-noticeable submersible, loaded to the plimsoll line with cameras and sample-collection gear, along with a crane to lower it from the deck of the ship into the water. Unofficially, there is a second submersible hidden inside the ship. A completely different design. One a tad more military in nature. Due to its small size, its weaponry is nothing to boast about. That said, it is stealthy in the extreme, so it should be able to maneuver close enough to the intruder to carry out an effective attack."

"So, I expect I'll be going out as a crewmember on this expedition, wait for the decoy sub to draw the intruder's attention, then use the stealth sub to go down and—what?"

"Poke a hole in its nethers. Not big enough to destroy it, but rather enough to make it leave the area in order to effect repairs—long enough to put the launch out of danger, in any case. Once you stick it with a pin, and it gets underway, we can arrange for an American Navy submarine to 'find' it and chase it out of the area. And perhaps force it to give us a clew as to who sent it and what its actual intentions were."

"One problem," I said. "I've never served on a sub. I don't know anything about them."

"The crew will take care of the operation of the submersible. You will be breveted as the mission commander and photo-recon officer. The submersible's Captain will still outrank you. Your orders will be carried out—but only insofar as the safety of the crew and the vehicle is not jeopardized."

"So," I said. "Back in the saddle again…"

"Indeed," she said. She took a bite of the stuffed crab. "One could wish for a dash or two of malt vinegar with this. Not quite fish and chips, but I could grow to like this. How do they prepare the stuffing? Do you know?"

"I think the little green bits are finely-diced Bell pepper," I replied. "From the taste of it, I suspect there is some onion and celery chopped up in there too. Probably some sort of creole spices from New Orleans, for flavoring. There are probably regional variations from all over the US, so what you get here will be slightly different from what you could expect in New Orleans or New York or San Francisco. It's good, though. Isn't it?"

"Excellent," she said, taking another bite. "I can get you to the expedition's ship tomorrow morning, bright and early. It isn't far from here—just down the coast, actually. A private research organization affiliated with several Universities and a television documentary studio in California. Also loosely affiliated with us, as well as your CIA."

"I see," I said. Now I understood why Joe was pretending to be an FBI agent. The CIA isn't supposed to operate inside the US—not openly, anyway. Still, Spooks are always gonna be Spooks. Also went a good way to explain Joe's casual disregard for having that cop beaten up. That was gonna haunt me. For a long time.

"In any case, Mister Darby," she said. "It seems our paths will continue to run parallel—at least for the rest of the night. So, what does a girl do for fun in this town?"

"Call me Tom," I said.

"Jill," she replied. "Jill Saunders."

"Pleased to meet you Jill," I replied with a smile. "As for nightlife in Daytona, it's mostly bar-hopping, restaurants, maybe dancing at a nightclub. However, I have to warn you that I'm not a very good dancer. The biggest attraction in this town is spending the days on the beach doing nothing, soaking up the sun, getting drunk, and hooking up with attractive members of the opposite sex."

"Sounds a bit like Brighton," Jill said, flashing me an encouraging smile. "Once we finish off this lovely shrimp and crab, what say we do a bit of pub-crawling for afters?"

"We can go up and down the boardwalk the rest of the afternoon," I replied. "I walked here from my motel—I don't like to ride my bike once I've had any beer, so I left it there."

"I took a taxi from my hotel," she said. "Walking seems to be the order of the day, then."

"Shall we explore?" I asked.

"Sir," she replied, smiling. "You interest me strangely."

A few minutes later, we left the restaurant and began walking up and down the boardwalk. The breeze from the beach was just strong enough to keep us from feeling overheated from the sun. The salt in the air cleared my head a bit from the beer buzz. We went into several tourist shops, had an ice cream cone from a vendor with a cart there on the boardwalk, and kept walking. The evening drew close and we hit several bars, had another meal, a few more drinks—she even persuaded me to dance with her in one club. I hoped I wasn't too awkward or embarrassing. Later that night we ambled hand in hand back up towards my motel. I had a pleasant glow from all the booze. I offered to call a taxi to get her back to her hotel, as I was unlocking the door to my room.

"Nonsense," she replied, and then she kissed me.

"You sure about this?" I asked when we paused for breath. "You've only just met me today."

"We're in *this* business, we've been together all day, and you have *yet* to make a pass at me," Jill replied. "And you offered to call for a taxi to take me to my hotel. You're not the least bit forward, are you?"

"No, Ma'am," I replied. "I'm actually very quiet and shy. Sort of awkward, too, as you may have noticed."

"I find that rather endearing," Jill said. "Tom, would you like some company tonight, or are you going to be chivalrous and send me away?"

"If you're going to be all polite about it," I said. "Then I'd like nothing more than the pleasure of your company tonight."

"That's settled, then," she said as she closed and locked the door for me. I turned off the room lights. There was enough light from the hotel patio and swimming pool coming through the drawn curtains for me to see her— once my eyes adjusted. We kissed again. Before too long we were undressing each other. I can still remember her apricot perfume. It filled my head and made me even drunker than the booze had done. She giggled as we laid down on the bed. And several times afterwards, as well. Eventually, we slept.

Daylight arrived altogether too soon to suit me.

"Want some tomato juice?" I asked as the morning sun lit the room and we each crawled out of bed. "Good for a hangover." Our clothes laid, ignored for the moment, on the floor next to the bed.

"That would be lovely," Jill said, standing up and stretching like a cat. "A bite of brekkie wouldn't be a bit amiss, either."

"I have eggs and sausage patties, and bread for toast in the fridge," I said as I walked over to the kitchenette corner of my room. "How do you like your eggs?" I added as I turned back to enjoy the view of her walking to the bathroom.

"I'm not picky," she said over her shoulder. "However you take them will be fine with me."

She didn't close the bathroom door, so I turned my back to give her some measure of privacy. After I poured us both a glass of tomato juice, I got my old mess kit out of my pack from where it stood on the kitchen floor. Unfolding the handle, I put it on one of the burners of the little motel stove. I grabbed four eggs, a stick of butter, a pint of buttermilk, sausage patties, and a loaf of bread from the fridge. Using another motel water glass from the cabinet, I cracked four eggs and dolloped them in, adding two ounces of buttermilk, a few dashes of salt and pepper, then used my trusty bamboo chopsticks to scramble the mix. I put a generous pat of butter into the mess kit frying pan, and turned the stove burner to Low. I popped two slices of bread into the toaster, but didn't start it yet. Toast is best if made just as the eggs are a moment or two away from being scrambled to perfection. I used the lid to the mess kit as a second frying pan, putting six sausage patties in and setting that burner to Low as well. It wouldn't hold any more, so six would have to do. I turned the heat up a bit, poured the eggs into the other pan, then turned its heat up a bit higher. From a pouch I kept in my pack, I got out my half-sized camp-gear spatula, a metal whisk, and both my folding sets of knife, fork, and spoon. I had some paper plates in the cabinet already, so I got two out, but I didn't need them just yet. I was glad I'd stopped at a grocery store on my way to my motel room, even if juggling a grocery sack on a motorcycle was a little tricky in downtown Daytona traffic. I'd done it before on the base, so I'd had some practice. I was using the whisk on the eggs as they slowly cooked, and flipping the sausages with my other hand when I felt a pair of feminine arms encircle my waist. She snuggled up close to my bare back. I could feel her skin against mine, from my hips to my shoulders. An inquisitive hand went exploring. Then another.

"If you keep that up, I'm not gonna be able to cook," I said.

"I've never seen anyone cook using both hands at the same time before," Jill said.

"I'm a pilot," I said. "Takes both hands and both feet to fly a plane."

"You just keep doing what you're doing," Jill replied. "I'm not touching your hands—or your feet…"

"It's time to start the toaster," I said, a moment later. "If you'd be so kind?"

"If you insist," Jill sighed, released one hand, and leaned over to push the bar down on the toaster. Then she put her hand back where it had been. Several long moments later, the second pair of toast slices were on the paper plate alongside the first, and I was placing sausage patties and scrambled eggs on them as well. She let me put the pans and other gear in the sink to wash up later, then stopped distracting me long enough for us to eat. After I had done the washing up and returned my mess gear to my pack., we took a shower. She found an entirely different way to distract me then.

"Leave your pack in the motel," she said as we got dressed. "You won't need it in the submersible. I'll ride with you on your motorcycle, so we don't have to go back to my hotel to fetch my car."

"This should be interesting," I said. "What about changes of clothes on the boat?"

"Our unit should have had a package delivered to the Institute by now, with everything you would need. Clothes, shaving kit, shoes, hat—"

"Ammunition?" I asked.

"You won't need that under water," Jill replied.

I picked up the canvas bag with my Colt and spare magazines, but I didn't tell her what was inside. "Every time I've been told I wouldn't need extra ammo," I said. "I wound up needing plenty. Are you ready?"

"Never ridden on a motorcycle before," Jill said. "This should be interesting."

"Just wrap your arms around my waist, hug yourself up to my back, and lean exactly the same amount in the same direction as I do," I said. "You'll have to talk loudly," I added as I put my leather jacket on. "And NO distractions!"

"Spoilsport," Jill said, as she faked a pout. We locked the room behind us and went to the motel carport for my bike. That's one of the reasons I like this place—roofed-in parking is ideal for motorcycles. Not many motels can boast that. Plus, the place is affordable.

I flipped the passenger foot pegs down for Jill, saddled up, then got her situated behind me. She wrapped her arms around my waist again, then I hit the electric starter and let the Harley warm up for a moment.

"Hang on," I said as I tapped the gear shifter into first. She hugged me tighter as I took us out of the carport and headed for the main drag.

"Go South," Jill said. So I did. Once out of the city limits, she gave me more directions. "It's about 25 miles, on the left. You'll see the sign. Littlejohn Research Institute for Oceanographic Studies. Turn in at the second driveway. That one goes to their pier."

"Do I have any cover identity for this, or am I just me?" I shouted back over my shoulder.

"Smith," she shouted back. "Doctor John Smith, from the University of Georgia."

"Oh, cute," I said under my breath.

"What?" Jill asked.

"Doctor of what?" I shouted back.

"Close," she replied, then giggled. "Geology and Archeology! Specializing in sonar mapping of the seafloor! Your pet project is finding Atlantis!"

"That's actually a thing?" I shouted back.

"I'm to be one of your Grad Students, working on my own degree!" Jill shouted back. "That way I can do most of the talking when someone asks inconvenient questions you can't answer! If anyone asks you anything, you look wise and ask me to explain, as if you are testing me!"

By this time I had the bike up to 65. The highway was empty. Cars were in the other lane going north, but we had the southbound lane to ourselves. I twisted the throttle a little more, and we hit 70. We passed through a short stretch of hurricane-damaged hotels and motels between the highway and the beach. Only their North and South walls were standing. Roofs gone, interior walls gone, East and West walls gone, just empty shells. Quicker than I expected, we reached a little town and saw the sign for the Littlejohn Institute. I slowed way down and looked for the driveway. The Institute itself looked like it was made of coral and seashells, like one of those old Spanish forts. I found the driveway and turned in, idling my speed down as I went down the short road to their pier. I reached a parking lot and pulled in. Once I parked the bike, we dismounted and Jill ran her fingers through her windswept hair. I grabbed my kit out of the saddlebags, pocketed the key, and turned to her.

"Do I need to bluff my way through any security checkpoints?" I asked her.

"Just walk up to that little guard shack over there, and introduce yourself as Doctor John Smith, and ask if Professor Littlejohn is available," Jill said. "Our unit should have arranged everything. Littlejohn is one of our 'friends.' He'll be nearby and walk us through any other security."

"Flimsiest set-up I've ever seen," said.

"They're actually not," Jill replied. "It's simply that we are expected and Littlejohn is part of the arrangement. Without him, you'd be amazed at how fast you'd be intercepted and carted off in police custody."

"Let's do this," I said. I shouldered my kitbag and she grabbed the smaller kit she'd put in the other saddlebag before we left the motel.

"After you, Doctor," she replied. We walked to the little guard shack. As we got close, a tall string-bean of a guy, wearing a monocle, stepped out of the scant shade the shack offered and waved us closer.

"Doctor Smith, I presume?" he said as we got close enough for casual conversation. "I'm exceedingly pleased that you could take time out of your busy schedule to join my little expedition." He removed his monocle and tucked it into a shirt pocket. "And this must be your assistant, Jillian."

I found myself adopting a Knoxville accent as I replied. "Thank you for taking the time to meet us, Professor. Are there any formalities we need to undergo before we board your research boat?" Educated Southern is how I thought of that accent. Just enough twang to be recognized as Tennessee, and just enough posh to be taken for city-folk.

"Indeed not," he replied. His accent was more Northern than mine. Boston or New York, but old school and decidedly more 'professor-ish' than mine. This guy had a *real* education. "Your University has provided us with your impeccable credentials aforehand. Shall we dispense with the formalities and go aboard? Oh, by the by, your equipment arrived this morning and is already loaded onboard, in your cabin. Arrangements have been made for Miss Jillian to accompany you, as per your request. You will have both an upper and lower bunk. I'll leave it to yourselves to sort out who gets which. Breakfast is at six, luncheon at noon, dinner at nine. The Galley and Wardroom are forward. The Head is amidships, I'm afraid. You will perforce need to work out a convenient schedule with your peers. George, wave us through, if you would be so kind."

George had to be the little old man in the khaki security guard uniform. I saw his arm move, his hands out of sight behind the windows of the guard shack, and the gate rose up. We walked through, and the professor turned to me again.

"You have spent some considerable time in Oak Ridge, I perceive," he said. "Regional dialects are a little hobby of mine. I would also hazard a guess that you have family from the Smoky Mountains region?"

"Quite a considerable bit," I answered. "To both, actually. My grandmother's house in LaFollette was close enough to the foothills of the Smokies that it looked as if you could reach out through the kitchen windows and touch them." That was my training kicking in. Jill's crash course on my cover story--and my ability to lie with a straight face. One of my spook-instructors was an acting coach, after all.

"My early schooling was in Clinton, just North of Knoxville," I added. "But I have traveled extensively."

"Yes," said Littlejohn. He smiled briefly, as if to tell me he was in on the joke. "Quite the globe-trotter, I'm given to understand."

This guy was smooth! Not only did he just tell me he'd read my file from Military Intelligence, but that he was comfortable with my assignment to his little team. I'm betting that he could carry though an innocent conversation with covert messages using the right word, and *just* the right inflection, at the perfect moment. I made a note to myself to *never* play poker with this man! We started up the gangplank to the research ship. I took it all in as I looked around. It wasn't a huge ship, but larger than

I expected. The bright yellow mini-sub for the public part of the operation was in a cradle in the middle of the deck. The stern had markings on it that I recognized as a landing pad for a small helicopter. The bow was longer than I had ever seen on a boat this size, and looking to the waterline I could make out a glass bubble, like an observation blister on a bomber, just under the waterline. The whole thing was longer and wider than I had ever seen on the Jacque Cousteau TV shows I'd watched. I guessed that was both for greater stability at sea and to hide the spook-sub Jill told me was inside the ship.

"Now, about your duties," Littlejohn added as we reached the main deck. "You will find your photography workstation on the lower deck, amidships. Our *probe* has the latest in low-light and infrared cameras—both movie and still, and the workstation control panels should already be familiar to you. We used a standardized instrumentation we borrowed from the Air Force—it was the most efficient design, we felt. Furthermore, the infrared spotlights should be totally invisible to *most* undersea life we should trust to encounter."

Those carefully inflected words told me the photo-recon station on the secret sub was laid out like ones I'd used before while I was flying jets. And that the powers that be considered their replacement for undersea spotlights to be undetectable by the target enemy sub. Once again, Professor Littlejohn had impressed me with his subtlety. *Forget poker,* I thought, *I ain't even playing tidily-winks with this guy!*

"I will no doubt need to take some time to familiarize myself with the camera controls," I said.

"You'll have an entire day in which to do just that," said Littlejohn. "We're not exactly equipped for speed. Our little *Lorelai* is more of a tugboat than a speedboat. She'll do 10 knots at best, laden as we are. We'll be at the point where we wish to release our little two-man diving saucer, over there." The professor pointed at the yellow-painted mini-sub in its cradle. "We call her *Lamia*, one of Poseidon's daughters."

"A queen of Libya, as I recall," said Jill.

"Exactly so," the professor replied. "By way of continuing that theme, your workstation has been nicknamed *Despoena* after another of Poseidon's daughters. The goddess of certain Arkadian Mysteries. She was a daughter of Poseidon and Demeter."

"Well, perhaps we will delve into a mystery tomorrow, then," I said.

Jill looked as if she wanted to kick my shin for that little pun. Then she smiled. *I'm gonna pay for that one later,* I thought. I smiled right back at her.

"I'll show you to your cabin," said Littlejohn. "Then I must have a word with Captain Jacobs as to when we can expect the rest of our crew to arrive. Once I am free, I will escort you below decks and let you begin to familiarize yourself with the photographic equipment controls."

The professor led us through a short maze of doorways and stairs until we reached a nondescript cabin door. There was no window in the door, and from the looks of the rubber seals around it, it was watertight. And hopefully soundproofed, so Jill and I could talk without being overheard.

"I'll leave you be for the nonce," Littlejohn said as he opened the door for us. "The Head is five doors aft if you need to shower or whatever. I'll knock you up later on. Make yourselves comfortable." Without another word, he left back the way we'd come.

"You are a smart ass," Jill said once we'd closed the door.

"Says so on the label," I replied. "What was that about special equipment? Did the unit send something over that I need to know about?"

"Probably just clothes and things," Jill replied. "Doesn't look like a large crate. I doubt it'll hold much." She pointed to the footlocker-sized shipping crate between the frame of the bunks and the forward wall.

"Doesn't look like it's been tampered with," I said as I took a close look at it. "Shall we open it?"

"Why not?" she replied.

I used the little crowbar that was sealed inside a plastic envelope taped to the top of the crate to get the lid off. Looked like clothes, some special gear in smaller boxes, and something resembling a very small, metal briefcase.

"Swimsuits and casual clothes," Jill said. "For both of us. These bikinis look like something Bettie Paige would wear. All right, this box has a little revolver in it, and ammo." She lifted the briefcase out of the way and put it on the lower bunk to get it out of the way, then started opening the other boxes. "This one is a box of .45 cartridges. Looks like they're coated with wax."

"Probably some kind of waterproofing," I said. "Right size for my Colt, though. I hope this doesn't mean that someone in Ops believes I'm going to have to use it underwater. Bugger is hard enough to clean as it is."

"The revolver is a .38 snubby," she said. "Two-inch barrel."

"Probably for you," I replied. "I can't hit the broad side of a barn with one. I'd only use it if I was standing next to a target. What else?"

"Knives. Looks like British paratrooper knives," Jill said. "Good if you need to stab someone up close and personal.

Thin as a razor and damned near as sharp. What's this thing? Looks like a SCUBA mouthpiece, with little bitty bottles attached."

"I've seen those before," I said. "SCUBA gear, but with a ten-minute air supply. Emergency gear only. Can't hook them up to regular-sized air tanks."

"Well," Jill replied. "At least there are two of them. This box has little flashlights, and some nylon headbands. Bright little buggers."

"Probably little pockets in the headbands to hold the flashlights," I said. "So you can go hands-free. Anything else?"

"Plastic explosives and detonators with timers. Four of each. And what is in these little test tubes?" Jill asked.

"Put those back GENTLY," I said. "Those are our final failsafe self-destruct option. That's a poison. VERY fast-acting. That crap makes cyanide look like an aspirin. One gulp of that, and three seconds later you're a corpse. Then your body starts dissolving. Head first. That is some nasty shit. You don't even need to drink it. Rub it on your skin and it works about ten seconds slower, but you are still dead. Someone thinks we're—"

"In danger of being captured by the Communists?" Jill asked.

"Or worse. OK, let's open the briefcase," I replied.

"Briefing papers?" Jill asked once we unlocked the case.

"Not the good kind," I said. "Vacuum-sealed in plastic? See the black edging on that stack? And the red edging on these? That's way beyond Top Secret stuff. Do you see any surgical gloves in the crate?"

"Two pairs," Jill replied. "Why?"

"Put one pair on, hand me the other pair. Red means they are classified as "burn after reading." Black means that the paper is poisoned. Once we open these packets? We've got—maybe half an hour before these things need to be off the ship, then they ignite on their own. And if we're still reading when the black ones light up, we're dead. These things were treated with a special mix of chemicals after they were printed. I've only seen this kit once before in my life, and that was really bad."

"Holy shite, Tom!" Jill said. "What have you gotten me into?"

"Welcome to my life, Honey," I said, pulling on the surgical gloves. "I'll take the black ones, you take the red. Let's start reading."

"Holy—," Jill whispered. "Darby, you are dangerous to know."

"Gloves on?" I asked.

"For God's sake, YES!"

"Let's read—" I replied. So, we started studying the documents provided. I hoped we got finished before the paperwork killed us.

Twenty-nine and a half minutes later we put the papers back into the briefcase, along with both pairs of gloves, opened our cabin's porthole, and shoved the briefcase overboard. Thankfully, it fit through the porthole. Once I heard the splash of the case hitting the water, I closed the porthole and dogged it closed.

"That's crazy," said Jill.

"It fit through the porthole," I said. "That was well planned. OK, brief me on the red and I'll brief you on the black."

"Whoever wrote what I read believes that the foreign sub we're supposed to run off is wanting to start a three-way nuclear war between the Russians, the Chinese, and the US and NATO alliance ," said Jill. "They doubt that it is the Communists, and they know it isn't us. They're making ready for Armageddon—all out nuclear war between the communists and everyone else. Everything's armed and ready to launch. Every ICBM, every bomber, every fighter, every army we have on this side of the Iron Curtain is prepared to launch in less than a minute's notice. They believe this weird sub we're after is supposed to drop that US orbital nuclear platform tomorrow—loaded with dozens of bombs, onto Cuba—just to start World War Three. And whoever owns that damned sub—they honestly think they can survive that? Where? How? And do what? Rule a dead planet?"

"Who knows?" I asked. "The black pages said that it was doubtful anyone would survive, no matter where or how deep their bomb shelters were. Not Asia, not Africa, not Siberia, not even Australia. Even submarine crews a mile deep wouldn't provide enough shelter to keep anyone alive long enough to even *try* to repopulate the world, Not after *that* much radioactive dust got thrown into the air. The radiation just lasts too long, the dust and smoke does too much climate damage. If that's what they intend, they're going to kill the entire human race. The black pages called it 'Nuclear Winter.' A thousand years of cold and smoke and dust, a new ice age, glaciers down to Guatemala or Kenya, hundreds of feet of snow all along the equator, for centuries! The only possible survivors would be cockroaches and ants!"

"So—what do we do?" Jill asked. Her voice cracked a little bit. I could tell she was scared. For that matter, so was I.

"We do the job," I replied. "I go out to identify that sub, and poke a torpedo into it tomorrow to convince it to get out of range of the launch. Or at least keep it distracted long enough to keep it from starting a war. You stay on the boat and make sure no one aboard tries to sabotage the mission. I know they're all supposed to be friendlies, but—"

There was a knock on the door. Jill put the top back on the crate of gear as I stood up and straightened my tie. She gave me a thumbs-up and I went to answer the door. It was the professor.

"We're almost ready to leave the dock," he said. "All the crew is onboard and the cook has announced dinner shall be served while we leave the harbor. If I may be so kind as to direct you to the wardroom?"

"Sounds heavenly," I said. "Jillian, are you ready?"

"Ready as I'll ever be," she replied. "Shall we go through?"

At dinner I met the rest of the crew—both public and secret. The two researchers going out in the *Lamia* were Bill and Ed, evidently college buddies from California. Blonde, blue-eyed surfer boys, both of them. Both had Bachelor's degrees and were working toward their

Master's. Bill in Marine Biology and Ed in some sort of Naval Engineering related to designing submarines for research work. I'm not sure I understood that correctly, but I could ask Jill later. There was a scientist from France studying several rare species of octopus. There was also an Italian lady lady who specialized in dolphins and whales. There was an older gent from Egypt whose specialty was ocean currents and had some sort of degree in underwater archeology and a young fellow from India who was the closest thing the ship had to a medical doctor. He was working through his Master's with an eye towards becoming a surgeon.

More important to me were my new partners on the *Despoena* mission for tomorrow. Jack and Trace. Jack was a retired Navy man who served on subs half his life. 60, if he was a day old. Crew cut, white moustache, five-foot ten, looked like he could bench-press a Buick. From the conversation we carefully tiptoed around, I gathered that he was the secret sub's Captain.

Trace was the most heavily muscled man I had ever seen, ex-Navy Seal, five-foot-tall, looking damn near that wide, and the blackest black man I have ever seen. I knew lots of black guys in the service, but they were all way more brown or cream-colored. Trace was so black his skin looked almost blue. As I understood it, he was Despoena's co-pilot and engineer. I felt like they were brothers of mine almost as soon as I heard them talk. They made it really hard to keep pretending I was a scientist. I could tell that they knew why I was really on the boat. But they played it cool. Not a hint that I was also one of the Brotherhood. All the dinner conversation really seemed like the young guys were flirting with Jill and the Italian lady while the rest of us were trying to pretend that we weren't here to stick a pin in some mysterious, probably enemy, submarine. Oh, Professor Littlejohn led a lot of the conversation concerning underwater archaeology and marine life, and from his voice, I could tell he was having fun dropping double and triple entendres only he was smart enough to fully understand. Those of us not children understood part of his jokes. The kids? Not so much.

After dinner, the professor offered to walk Jill back to our cabin so that I could go with Jack and Trace to check out the photo-recon equipment "belowdecks." She shot me a look I didn't understand. I knew it had to be something between "be careful" and "I'll keep the light on for you," but I haven't had *that* much experience with women, so I just didn't know. I just smiled and nodded and hoped she knew I didn't have the slightest idea what she was trying to tell me.

Jack and Trace led me to a ladder inside what appeared to be a janitor's closet. The door was locked so no one on the crew but them could open it. Once we were inside the secret sub *Despoena,* Jack turned to me and said "Captain, guard this with your life," and handed me a key to the closet door.

Despoena had three seats, was cramped, and my eyes lit up when I saw the photo-recon station. I knew the layout well from my days and nights flying for the spooks. It looked like half the control panels I had used solo on the old A12s. But in this case, Trace was the pilot, Jack was the Com-Ops, and all I had to do was run the cameras.

"You should know this gear," Jack said as he and Trace took their stations.

"Looks like some of the stuff from the spy-planes I used to drive," I said. "But updated."

"It is, but updated, like you said. Can you get the hang of it before dawn?"

"Rangefinder," I began, pointing to a display I knew well. "Five cameras—three still and two movie cameras—one real-time and one highspeed. I'm guessing these are the controls for exterior spotlights. Probably infra-red. The two screens that look like they ought to be radar are most likely sonar. Radar doesn't work underwater. I'm guessing one is active pinging and one passive recon. But Littlejohn hinted at something new and different in being able to take photos deep underwater. Unless that's something like that coherent light beam doohickey I read about that some geezer in Hawaii just invented, I haven't a clue. And *that's* a weapons control panel, or I'm a country mule. Torpedoes?"

"You'll do," Trace said over his shoulder. "Your accent shifted from Georgia Cracker to Virginia. Where are you from, Captain?"

"West Virginia, originally," I replied. "But I grew up all over the place. I flew Saber jets over Korea, back in the day. Wasn't old enough to be there legally. But the county courthouse burned down when I was ten, so I got away with lying about my age so I could enlist. No records of my birth. Served on the ground in the Army until I got into the Air Corps. Shot down a few MIGs, got noticed. Back before I sold my soul to the Spooks at Langley. They let me keep flying. Photo-recon and spy planes, then I got ground missions for the spooks when they needed someone to do an extraction on some team or other. I'm just a pilot. They keep trying to draft me into the Chair Force, but I'm too useful on the ground and in the air for it to stick. I hope we aren't gonna have a problem, 'cause I believe you could pick me up and rip me in half, Trace."

Jack and Trace both laughed.

"You'll do," said Jack. "OK, I'm the commander of this boat, Trace drives it, you take photos and when the time comes, you're Weapons Op. You've got an arsenal of five—count 'em, five torpedoes. All of 'em about as long as your leg and not even as big around as Trace's arms. They're extremely high-explosives for their size. They each have roughly the power of 1200 pounds of TNT. That's twice the power of a normal torpedo. These are beyond Top Secret. And they are damned expensive. They have very limited range, so if you pop one off, we're going to get a nosebleed. Aim *carefully!* Because they are so tiny, we have an effective range of 100 to 200 yards. The shockwave will be 'talk back to your momma' brutal. A normal-sized sub's torpedoes have a range of a quarter to half a mile. Or better. We don't have the option of a 'better.' You poke this dragon with one of our firecrackers, we're gonna get slapped into the middle of next month. Got that?"

"Yes Sir," I said. "Do these have timers? Or magnetic clamps? Can we get close, stick one up the dragon's ass, light the fuse, and run away?"

"You have a fine grasp of tactics, Captain." Trace said.

"Yes, yes, and yes we can," said Jack. "That's how we trained. Get just within range, fire, then run like hell."

"I have no problem with that," I replied. "I've run like hell after taking photos with an A-12. Had to dodge more surface to air missiles than many a sane airman. You want 'Cool Hand Luke,' then I'm your man."

"OK, let's run a simulation," said Jack. "Training exercise."

"Go," I replied. "Let's do this thing."

Hours later, I climbed the ladder and headed towards my cabin. Dawn was rapidly approaching and I needed a few, if not many, hours of sleep before this mission went live. Jill was asleep in the bottom bunk when I got into our cabin and locked the door. I debated taking the top bunk, but decided that I'd rather feel her next to me for what little remained of the night than possibly die tomorrow without feeling anything but cold bed sheets. I stripped off my clothes and climbed into the bunk with her. She was naked, warm, sound asleep, and feeling her skin against mine as I hugged her tight on what could well be the last night of my life—was probably the closest to Heaven I'll ever know. I fell asleep within moments, the faint scent of her perfume and the caress of her skin against mine the only thing on my mind.

The next day, after a good breakfast and a briefing for the public part of this mission, I watched the crew lower the yellow submersible into the water, frogmen detach the cables leading from the crane, and the diving saucer sank rapidly out of sight. I went back to the stealth sub with Jack and Trace to watch the scopes that were hooked up to the ship's sensors. True to the plan, the submersible was making itself highly obvious to the hidden sub sitting in the dark below us. Active sonar, spotlights, lots of whiny noise from its electric engines and sample collecting gear. After four hours, the yellow sub returned and was hoisted back into its cradle on the ship. The plan was for them to get eight hours sleep and do a night dive in their sub. That's when we would drop out of the bottom of the ship and do our own recon, under cover of darkness. Supper that evening, as darkness began to draw close, was much the same as the day before. Jill and the Italian lady got flirted with. The Professor cracked his subtle style of jokes. Trace and I and Jack found ways to talk about the equipment on the secret sub that sounded perfectly innocent to the scientists. Once the meal was over, the college boys went to get into their sub, the scientists split up to go to their own workstations, Jill and the Professor went up to see the diving saucer be launched. Jack, Trace and I were free to go unlock our closet and climb down into *Despoena*. We switched on all the sub's systems, strapped into our seats, and waited. Through the camera feeds from the ship and the *Lamia*, we watched as the diving saucer submerged, switched on her spotlights, and proceeded to play decoy.

When our turn came, a door slid open in the bottom of the ship and our little stealth sub silently dropped through it into the blackness of the Atlantic at night. I fired up the passive instruments and the infra-red lights. Jack and Trace worked together like they'd been partners for years. A quiet word, a nod, hand signals, that's all it took for them to get us down and towards the lurker in the deep. I kept a watch on the scopes. Once we left the ship, we couldn't see the live feed from the other cameras any more.

"Almost at max depth," Trace said. If I hadn't been sitting next to him, I wouldn't have heard him.

"Steady. Hold course and depth," Jack replied. Same quiet voice Trace used. These guys were good.

"Got a vague picture," I whispered. "This thing is big. No tail fins, no propellers—I can't even see a conning tower. What the hell is this thing?"

Jack looked over my shoulder at my instruments. "Looks like a whale without any fins," he said.

"Moby Dick here ain't got nothing like diving planes or fins," I replied." And from here, it looks like the stern has got big holes in it. Can't be torpedo tubes. Looks more like railway tunnels. I can't make out any markings with the IR. If this thing has paint on it, the paint is as cold as its skin. Orders, Captain Jack?"

"Keep your cameras rolling," Jack said. "Trace, get us a little closer to the stern. I want to know what those 'tunnels' are."

"Got all the cameras running, IR and passive sonar too," I replied.

"My money is on engines," Trace said. "Only, enclosed in the boat itself. Like a jet plane."

"I think you're right," I said. "Wonder what kind? Can you make a water jet work for a sub? I count seven tunnels, the center one is three times the diameter of the ring of six surrounding it."

"If it's nuclear," said Trace. "Damn thing is plenty big enough."

"How would that work?" I asked.

"Pull in water from the front," Jack replied. "Boil it into steam to drive turbines. Use those to push even more water out of the back. Need one hell of a filter system, though. Gotta keep fish and seaweed out of the system."

My IR scope lit up red—like a preacher in a whorehouse.

"Heat signatures, big ones," I said.

"They've seen us," said Jack. "Evasive action! Blow ballast and get us the fuck out of here, Trace!"

"We're not in range for a torpedo, Jack," I said.

"Damn the torpedoes!" Jack said.

"Copy, shutting down weapons systems" I replied.

Mud and sand swirled in the water and all my spy gear went blind.

"Going up!" Trace said.

Suddenly, I was very glad for the seat belts. We got spun around like a rock in a spin-dryer. Tail over teakettle and even upside down a few times. Jack's chair ripped from the deck and he slammed into the hull. Felt like a 2 G bank and climb to me. I heard bolts groan in my own chair, and saw Trace fighting the controls at his. Jack moaned loudly. I guessed he was still alive. God only knows how badly hurt he was, though. Trace looked over his shoulder at Jack where his chair had him pinned against the bulkhead.

"Thank god this damn thing's so small," Trace said. "He only went about three feet. Still, as hard as he hit, he's gonna have a concussion."

"I've got some first aid training," I said. "Not a lot, but hopefully enough. I'll see to Jack while you get up to the surface. Is the boat all right? Are YOU all right?"

"I think my right arm is broken," Trace said calmly. "Bone ain't stickin' out though. I'm havin' to do everything left-handed. How's Jack?"

"I've got him out of the seat straps," I said. "Laid him out on the deck. He's got one hell of a goose egg on his noggin, but his breathing is all right and his pulse is steady. What do I do with the damned seat?"

"Kick it out of the way as best you can. I'm gonna need you to take over my chair. I can't steer this thing with a broken arm."

I blinked.

"I hope you're a damn good coach," I said. "'Cause I ain't never driven a submarine before."

"You goin' all cracker on me again," Trace replied, then laughed.

"Yeah," I replied. "You can take the boy off of the farm, but you can't take the farm out th' boy."

We both laughed. Trace unstrapped and moved to my seat. I snapped Jack's seat belts on his empty seat around a handhold next to the ladder tube.

"That'll keep the chair from hitting him if I don't get good *really* fast," I said as I strapped into Trace's chair at the sub's controls.

"I read your file," Trace said as he made a sling out of his belt, to support his broken arm. "At least, the parts that weren't classified above my clearance." He grunted in pain as he got his arm into a more comfortable position. "You can fly anything they ever put you into, and more. You stole a MIG in Korea. You stole a captured Starfighter back from the Russians. You *redlined* an A-12 to get away from a surface to air missile! Gossip in the unit is that you've flown faster than anyone in the world who isn't an astronaut. You're good."

"Only thing I'm good at is saving my own ass," I replied absently as I looked over Trace's control panel.

"That's why I want you in my chair," Trace replied. "So save yo' ass--and save ours too, while you're at it. The ballast lever is the yellow one over by your left hand. Throttle is the three sliders by your right. Pull back on the yoke to angle up, forward to dive. Turn the yoke for left and right, same with the foot pedals. Foot pedals are coarse controls, the yoke is fine control. Both together are big turns; yoke alone is tiny turns. Push the ballast lever up one notch for every fifty feet we go up. Be gentle with that or we'll need a decompression chamber when we reach the surface. Pull back on the yoke and push the throttles to three quarter power. Nice and easy. We may have knocked some rivets loose and we damn sure don't want to spring a leak!"

"Sir! Yes Sir," I said as I began our accent.

Four terrifying hours later, I got the sub parked in its bay on the ship, and the door between us and the briny deep closed.

"When I get back to Daytona," I said. I am going to drink EVERY beer in town!"

"Save some for me, Captain," said Trace. He laughed, winced because his broken arm moved, then clapped me on the back with his good arm. A medic climbed down and started strapping Jack into a lift sling on a rope and pulley arrangement to get him up the ladder. Jack opened his eyes, blinked a few times, then added "I'm in, but you two owe me a bottle of whiskey."

"That can be arranged," I said, grinning at Trace.

I had a private chat with the Professor later. Jill was there too, but no one else. We were in the Professor's private cabin—with the door locked and Jill standing next to it with her little .38 in her hands."Did you make out anything useful from the instrument recordings?" I asked.

"Very little," said Littlejohn. "Oddest design for a submersible that I have ever seen. The way it powered up and ran away is like no technology the UN or NATO has on record. We might see more once the films have been developed—but somehow, I doubt we will be able to trace its owners. The Russians have nothing like it, neither do the Chinese. I will file a full report with your superiors once we have all the film in hand. I doubt you will have to do more than file a more formal report to Major Jones of what you witnessed firsthand, once you return to your base in California. As of my last communique to your CIA, this matter has been *highly* classified. Your base commander might request to sit in on your debriefing with Major Jones, but I doubt he will avail himself of the opportunity."

"How is Jack?" I asked. "And Trace?"

"Jack is recovering nicely," said Littlejohn. "Minor concussion, no broken bones. Our doctor ordered him to his cabin to rest up. Trace has his arm in a sling, but should heal fairly quickly. He's a good, strong young man. No other injuries at all. He told me to compliment you on your piloting skills, by the by. I do believe you managed to impress both he and Jack."

"What is your best guess on that submarine?" Jill asked.

"I hesitate to speculate," replied the Professor. "I haven't enough evidence. However, I can draw a minimum of inferences. Since no one has ever encountered anything like it before, I would venture to say that it is the only vessel of its kind, so far. Its speed, maneuverability, and stealth gives me to reason that whoever owns and operates it has been acting in secret for an extremely protracted time. It cannot be the first of its kind to have been built. But its developmental stages have been carried out in utmost secrecy. Moreso than any flavor of Communists have been able to successfully achieve so far—in all of their history. Whoever built it must be extremely wealthy. They must also have carried out their experiment's development far away from the usual haunts of the US Navy, or the Soviet and Chinese Navies as well. If I were a betting man, I would say that it was developed in the Indian Ocean, quite possibly closer to Antarctica than anywhere else. Other than that, it could just as well have fallen out of the sky, for all I can tell."

"We are headed back to the institute?" Jill asked. "I can feel the ship is underway."

"Yes," replied Littlejohn. "We should dock shortly before dawn."

"What do we do now?" I asked.

"You return to your well-earned vacations," said Littlejohn. "I took the liberty of requesting that your leave be extended for both of you. Your commander agreed., Captain. As did your Supervisor, Miss Saunders. Now, both of you, go get some sleep. Pack up that crate of special gear tomorrow after breakfast. Once we disembark, and you are safely away from the Institute, I will arrange for it to be returned to the unit's Special Sections quartermasters. Oh, I am informed that your Supervisor wishes you to retain possession of that revolver, Miss Saunders. When you return to duty, you will be assigned a schedule for firing range times to practice with it. I would not be unduly surprised if there were a promotion in your near future. Now, go get some sleep. I'm tired, myself."

We left. When we got back to our cabin, Jill found an entirely new way to surprise me. We spent the night in each other's arms.

Two days later, the party was epic. But I never *did* find out what that damned submarine was. I spent the next two weeks with Jill, enjoying Daytona, enjoying each other's company. When we said our goodbyes, I never thought I would see her again. Maybe I would, maybe I wouldn't. Only time would tell.

I got back on my bike and headed back to base in California. I went North towards Atlanta so I could take

Highway 20 back West. I didn't want to run into that cop again.

I still wonder about him, sometimes…

Mission: Improbable

"I got moved around a lot, Advanced Training and all.
Some days, I wished I'd stayed on the farm…"
— Tom Darby.

By 08:55 I was in the Base Commanders outer office. His secretary, a young Corporal, had taken my name and told me to be seated. Once I sat, he ignored me. At 09:00 on the dot, the intercom signaled that the Commander was ready for me to go through. I was still in civvies when I walked through the door. I'd only just arrived back on base when I got the call. The training mission had gone passably well, but I still wasn't happy with my performance. The General waved me to a seat between an Admiral and an Air Force General. No one offered coffee, so I figured this was going to be more of a dressing down than a debriefing. A quick glance around the room revealed a well-dressed elderly man who was also in civvies. He nodded at me as soon as I noticed him.

"Captain," the General began. "Your training exercise will have to be cut short. Something has come up that you are best suited to deal with. By the way, nice shooting back there in the training village. If your assessors hadn't been wearing body armor, all four would be either dead or in hospital for months. Michaels will be wearing a cast for some time, but the doctors tell me he will regain full use of his shoulder in a matter of months. I will make note that the ammunition you were issued is slightly 'overpowered' for training, and we'll say no more about it. Our fault, not yours. On the evidence, quarter-loads are still too strong."

"Perhaps we could switch to training weapons that fire capsules of paint or some kind of dye?" I asked. "Wouldn't have the same recoil as real firearms, but a splat of paint shouldn't put anyone in the infirmary. Just a suggestion, Sir."

"Noted, and an excellent suggestion. I'll put it to the research department. You do play rough, young man."

"Sorry Sir. Only way to stay alive out in the field—or so I've found. Shoot first, shoot fast, hit the target, and don't hang around long enough to hear any questions be asked. My apologies to the assessor team."

"Also noted. Now, as I said, we have need of someone with your skills. Hypothetically, what would you say would be the best way to get a small team into hostile territory to recover a scientist and his immediate family who wishes to defect to our side?"

"How many family members, from where, and how small a team?" I asked. "This is need to know intel for mission planning, Sir."

"Very good," said the Air Force General. The Admiral nodded in agreement. The old man in civvies nodded, too.

"A Chinese scientist and his teenage daughter," the Base Commander said. "They are currently in Cuba. Castro 'liberated' them from his Russian allies. They are currently being well treated and the Russians and Cubans have no idea we have been in contact with the scientist."

"Tricky," I replied. "Back in the day I would have suggested infiltrating as tourists from a cruise ship, probably one owned by some Organized Crime syndicate. Nowadays that would be fairly difficult. Even the Mob would have trouble getting anyone in and out of there, now. Submarines are a possibility, but not a certainty. If we could get word to the scientist to take up an interest in deep sea fishing, that might get him and his daughter off-shore far enough for a SEAL team to board and get them off the boat to where a sub could extract them safely. Might have to sink the fishing boat as a cover, though. What are the weather predictions for any windows of opportunity?"

"You do think sideways, Son," said the old man in civvies. "I like that."

The brass in the room nodded as if the old man were someone they had to answer to, like a Congressman or something.

"Gentlemen," continued the old man. "I think the boy has the beginning of a workable plan. We should put steps in motion to get the Chinaman and his daughter out on a boat where the Admiral's subs can come into play. And we'll need the best weather reports of any storms forming once the plan is in motion. Timing will be of the essence."

"Hurricane season is coming up soon," said the Admiral. "If we can get the scientist to go fishing a few times before then, and let the Cubans bring him back while we prepare, when we finally make the extraction, they should be complacent, unsuspecting. I can have a sub and crew ready to go whenever we decide it's time."

"I can schedule a distraction on the far side of Cuba," said the Air Force General. "Something to keep Castro looking the other way while we pull this off."

"Gentlemen," said the old man. "I suggest that the Captain and I go off and brainstorm a few ideas while you put wheels in motion. The scientist must be contacted and instructed to take up an interest in deep sea fishing. Once that habit is normal to the Cubans, we can advance to the next phase."

"Agreed," said the two Generals and the Admiral.

"Captain Darby," said the Base Commander. "You are hereby assigned to work with Doctor Smith until such time as the mission planning is completed. Dismissed."

I stood as the Brass left the room. I was alone with the old man. I looked at him and raised one eyebrow. "Doctor John Smith, I presume?" I asked.

"Ten out of ten, young man," he replied, then smiled. "Shall we go and get some breakfast while we get to work?"

Suddenly, he reminded me of my grandfathers, both of them, and my Dad too. He stood and swept out of the office, with me in his wake. I could see why the Brass were deferential towards him, even without knowing what rank or authority he might have. The old man was like a force of nature. Nothing could get in his way.

We went to the mess hall and got plates of eggs, bacon, biscuits, and gravy. It was odd, but he seemed to get the same things I liked. We used the same amount of salt and pepper, too, and both poured cups of strong, black coffee.

"Humph," he said. "No cantaloupe or honeydew melon. Not even a pineapple. At least the gravy smells right."

"You don't *sound* Southern, but you *eat* Southern," I said.

"Correct," he replied as he tore his biscuits in half, laid them back on his plate, and spooned gravy over them. "I've learned that culture is a state of mind, not necessarily a product of where one was born."

"I'll try and remember that," I replied.

"Mind you, some fried ham and redeye gravy wouldn't be a lick amiss. The Army seems to have forgotten that." He dug into his breakfast and so did I. "Coffee isn't bad, though," he added.

"I can't get the cooks to add in grits or hash browns," I said between bites. "They're Yankees. But they do bake good biscuits and don't do raw bacon."

"Ugh, the Brits are the worst for taking a nice slice of bacon and just waving it in the general vicinity of a frying pan," the old man said between bites.

I liked this guy already.

"I never could get used to baked beans and blood pudding as a part of breakfast," I said. "But a slice of tomato ain't never out of place."

"Ever go someplace where they put peas in your scrambled eggs?" asked the old man.

"Bristol, England,' I replied. "But they made up for that with mushrooms and thick-sliced potatoes on the side. Brits have a weird idea on what foods should go together. But I fell in love with Cornish Pasties when I was in Portsmouth. Beef and potatoes and carrots and onions, fried up in a pastry that looked like an apple turnover. I can believe that coal miners took those down for a meal in the mines. That was wonderful!"

"Now, pork pies," said the old man as he cleaned his plate. "If you don't have any mustard, those things taste like spam in a pie crust."

"Yeah, but you can't beat the English for making a pot roast dinner," I said. "Like Sunday dinner at Granny's. Everything, and more!" I finished off my breakfast, took a long swig of my coffee, and looked the old man right in the eye. "You've been around, ain't ya?"

"Kid," he replied. His hazel-green eyes bored into mine like spotlights. "Even if you had the clearance for me to tell you, you wouldn't believe a word of it. He laughed. "Have you got an office where we can go continue this?"

"No," I said. "But I have enough pull to opt out of the BOQ. I have my own bungalow over in Officer Country. Not much to speak of, but I don't have to share it."

"Not married?" He asked.

"In this business? I wouldn't want to leave a widow," I replied. "Shall we grab a jeep?"

"Sounds like a plan," he said. We left the mess hall and flagged down the first jeep that was going our way. Quicker than a greased pig, I welcomed the old man into my humble abode. At least I didn't have to apologize for any mess. I always kept the place clean enough to pass inspection. Once inside, I started a pot of coffee and we sat down at the table to get down to business. The longer I knew the old man, the more it seemed like I always had known him. I got out a pad of paper and a couple of pencils.

"How are we going to make this work?" I asked.

"You'll have the hard part, the extraction," said the old man. "I can't help you with that. I'm too old to get back out in the field. Just slow you down. I can help more from back here. Seeing to it you get all the support and equipment you need."

"I wouldn't be much use on a submarine," I said. "I sort of proved that a couple of years ago."

"Yes," said the old man. "But you've trained on SUCBA gear since then. You'd swim up with the extraction team, board the boat, help take care of any guards, and get the Professor and his daughter into the sub—once it was safe for the sub to surface."

"Listen," I interrupted. "Do I know you from somewhere? You seem familiar. Have we met before?"

"I've got the same sort of background as you," he replied. "Country boy, ran away from the family farm to join the Army. Impressed my superiors on the ground and the Spooks recruited me, eventually."

"Small world," I said. "But there's more to it than that, I'm sure."

"When I was younger," he said, "I lived in the same part of West Virginia as you. You might have seen me around. At the Feed and Seed, maybe a Church Revival meeting, maybe even fishing somewhere. I got around."

"I don't remember a Doctor Smith," I said.

"Cover identity," Smith said. "Back in the day, I was— Rufus Boone. That's a name I haven't used in a very long time. But keep calling me John Smith. I'm afraid that poor old Rufus died a long time ago, to protect my family."

"I understand," I said. "Funny, though… Rufus was my Daddy's name, and Boone was my Momma's maiden name. We might even be related, somehow."

"From West By-God Virginia? I wouldn't be a bit surprised," said the old man. He smiled, as if he knew a secret and wasn't *about* to let me in on it. I started wondering if he wasn't a cousin on my Momma's side. There had been a couple of birth records inked over in my Momma's family bible, on the genealogy pages. Momma always said those were a few Black Sheep from the family.

They'd got disowned—or some such. Wouldn't talk about it anymore, so I never knew the details.

"Now," Smith said, interrupting my thoughts. "Let's think of all the ways this can blow up in our faces, and make some plans just in case, shall we?"

"Well, the first thing that could go wrong," I said, "Cuba might not let the professor go fishing at all. Or they might let him, but not let him take his daughter along."

"Right, that's two," Smith replied as he wrote them down. "What else?"

"Getting the sub close enough, without being detected. Do we have a budget for a diversion of some kind?"

"Maybe," he said. "But it would have to be something believable. I'll talk with the Admiral and see if he has any ideas."

"Guards on the boat?" I asked.

"Most likely, a whole squad—the first few times," he replied. "But if he can make a habit of it, they might scale it back to one or two."

Smith scratched away at his notepad. "Someone is going to have to make sure the frogmen can climb aboard the boat," he said. "Deep sea fishing boats aren't small."

"The frogmen can't risk getting tangled up in the fishing lines," I said.

"Good point," Smith said as he made another note. My own notepad was still blank, except for a doodle that looked a little like an old airplane, and some spider-doodles. I don't know why I draw spiders when I'm trying to think. Maybe from sitting in the old outhouse, back on the farm, when I was a kid. Always had to check for widows before you sat down. Momma always warned me not to get my dangly bits bitten. Only thing that ever really scared me was that big rattlesnake I opened the door on when I was 12. Daddy got it with his shotgun, and made a hatband out of its hide, but he cussed about needing to patch the hole in the floor. There was always a box of sulfur powder to sprinkle around on the floor after that. Don't know if that's an old wives' tale or not, but we never had any other snakes in the outhouse after that.

"If it works," I said. "It works."

"What?" Smith asked.

"Just remembering life on the farm," I replied.

"Working the garden?" Smith asked. "Or hunting with your family, or emptying the chamber pot into the outhouse?"

"We really must be related," I answered. We both laughed.

"Anything's possible," he said,

"That Institute in Florida," I said. "The one I worked with a few years back. They had a little bitty sub designed to sneak up on things. It only held three people, though."

"What about it?" Smith asked.

"I wonder if they have a 5-seater now." I said.

"Valid point," Smith replied. "I can ask around. That would be a better cover than trying to get a Navy sub close enough to Cuba. They make TV documentaries, don't they?"

I looked at him and raised one eyebrow.

"I was briefed," he said—as if that were an answer.

"No one briefed me about you," I said.

"You don't have high enough clearance to be briefed about me," he replied. "I'm so far above Top Secret that they haven't even got a word for it yet. Half of the Big Brass think I just walked out of thin air." He grinned. "The other half think I can walk on water. Play this game long enough, you get a reputation. Ain't always a bad thing.

Ain't always good, either. Once that reputation gets around, you wind up with friends—and enemies—in some very high places. You get to break rules and intimidate some mighty powerful people. On both sides of the law. I once had to kill a man who wanted to start a nuclear war. Friend of mine, at the time—before he went crazy."

"Well, shit," I said.

"He was a US Senator, no less," said Smith in a sad voice. "Got ahold of the launch codes for SAC—was about to fake a Russian attack on the big computer screens in Cheyenne Mountain and impersonate the President on the Hot Line a few minutes later. I was standing right behind him as he started the fake-out. I cut his throat with a straight-razor. 1964, that was, about four months after Kennedy was shot in Dallas. I always thought he had something to do with the assassination, so I got into his inner circle to check him out. Had dinner with his family more than once. I had to get that close to get into his confidence. Aside from being a homicidal maniac, he was a pretty nice guy."

"Who?" I asked.

"Can't tell you," he replied. "Publicly, it was reported as a car wreck. Closed casket funeral, with Honor Guards and everything. Even his wife doesn't suspect a thing, to this day. I still send her Christmas cards. I stood in for him when his daughter got married and I walked her down the aisle to give her away to her husband. As far as they know, I was his best friend. Saving the world ain't always pretty, Kid. No way to keep your hands clean—not always. I went into deep cover after that. Always a different name, different identity, hiding in plain sight. The brass only sends for me now when the shit is just about to hit the fan. I'm so old no one expects me to be what I really am. It's like being the guy who taught James Bond how to be James Bond. The shadows are always the safest place to live."

I couldn't think of a thing to say.

"You about ready for lunch?" Smith asked, changing the subject.

"Yeah," I replied. "I only had time for a quick bite before the meeting this morning."

"Then let's go see if they have any pot roast, or some meatloaf and mashed potatoes over at the chow hall," he said. "I'm about to starve, myself."

We left my quarters and flagged down a passing jeep.

"Nice bike," he said as we walked past my motorcycle, parked outside my quarters, and looked for a ride.

"Thanks," I said as I flagged down a jeep headed in the right direction. "I bought it new, a few years back."

The Private in the jeep saluted both of us when he stopped. Smith's return salute was as perfect as if he'd been Army born and bred. He got saluted a few more times as we got out at the chow hall. He nodded instead of saluting back.

"I forgot they need to think I'm a civilian," he explained as he brushed dust off of his suit. "Anyone in civvies on a base could be some congressman, or something."

"That was a damned crisp salute you gave the Private who picked us up," I said. "When did you serve?"

"Same as you, Captain," he replied. "Same as you. Korea 'til now. I wasn't allowed to enlist for anything earlier. And the reason for that is classified, so don't ask. I was a Major when I retired. Got enough points on my record now to be a General—but I can't be one because of what I *do*. Paperwork is traceable. Shadows aren't. Let's eat, Boy! I'm about to starve."

We went through the line and both settled for almost the same thing. Fried chicken, mashed potatoes with brown gravy, slaw, biscuits, and a couple of slabs of butter for the biscuits. He got green beans, I got pintos. He tasted his tea and complained about how much sugar was in it. I got black coffee, but I wanted buttermilk. Not on the menu today.

We demolished our meals in near silence. "Food is for eatin'—not talkin' over," he said between bites. He went back for seconds. For an old man, he sure could eat. He was built like a Drill Sergeant anyway, but he reminded me of Daddy after a lifetime of farming. Might have had a little bit of a beer gut, but if he lifted a tractor off the ground, I wouldn't have blinked. Daddy had a way of making you believe he was Superman, and trying to hide it. Smith did too. I was beginning to like the old man.

Once we finished eating, he looked me in the eyes like Daddy used to do when he was about to tell me something I needed to pay attention to.

"The professor's daughter is 16, probably be 17 by the time we do this rescue," said the old man. "She might latch onto you as some kind of hero after saving her and her dad. Don't forget what your Momma told you about little girls. Don't lay a finger on her, even if she wants you to. Even if she tries to romance you. Protect her, protect her father, but she shouldn't ever be another notch on your bedpost. Don't let any of the sailors on the mission do it either. Even if you have to beat the crap out of a couple of them. This is important, Boy. You've been around. You know how to charm women into sharing your bed. This is a little girl who *hasn't* been around. If you take advantage of her affections, I will be *highly* disappointed in you."

His tone of voice promised a world of hurt if I disobeyed. Fortunately, Momma and Daddy didn't raise no fools. Nor did they raise boys who failed to respect women. And I was always taught to protect children. There was that time my younger sister beat the ever-living crap out of a football player who wouldn't take no for an answer on their second, and last, date. Me and my brothers wanted to go teach him the error of his ways, but Daddy wouldn't let us. The boy's family moved away right after he got out of the hospital. I hear he had a limp the rest of his life. He married once, but it seems he never had any kids. My sister Darla May Darby wasn't a girl to trifle with.

"Won't be a problem," I replied. The tone of my voice said you could take that to the bank. "I am a gentleman. Born and raised."

"Glad to hear it," Smith replied. "Now, let's go finish up planning this rescue and go see the Big Brass in the morning."

"Sir! Yes Sir!" I said. We left the chow hall and looked for another jeep going our way. The old man got saluted a few more times before a jeep stopped for us. We spent the rest of the afternoon and evening going over our plans as best we could, without knowing what sort of resources we could count on having. I was out of beer by the time we thought about sleeping.

He slept on my couch. Me, in my bunk. I woke up at dawn to find him already awake and showered and making a pot of coffee. We took a quick trip to the chow hall for eggs, bacon, hash browns, and sausage gravy ladled over biscuits. He'd made a few telephone calls the night before, and had several more pages of notes. I don't know how he did it, but we were ushered into a meeting with the same Brass we'd met with the day before, allowed access to the folks in Florida I had worked with on that unknown mystery submarine thing a few years ago, and given a blank check for expenses. Either this professor was really important, or the old man has more connections than the Madame of the most exclusive bordello I've ever heard about.

After meeting with the Brass, he and I went back to my quarters.

"The professor will be messaged about taking up fishing as a hobby," Smith told me. "Your friends at the institute do have a larger stealth sub now, and a bigger boat to hide it in. There's a Spanish shipwreck from the 1500s, near enough to Cuba for our purposes, that they are trying to get official permission to film with their little diving saucer. It's in prime fishing waters too. The only hold ups will be getting the professor's handlers used to the idea that he enjoys going fishing, getting Cuba to issue a permit for the film crew to take the Institute's boat there, and waiting for the professor's guards to get complacent with nothing ever happening on his fishing trips beyond their getting to eat fresh fish."

"How long will we have to wait?" I asked.

"Four months or so, probably," said Smith. "Six months would be better, and more in line with the Cubans issuing permits for the film crew to make their documentary in their waters."

"What about the little girl?" I asked. "He won't want to defect without his daughter. And whatever happened to his wife?"

"She died ten years ago," Smith said. "Pneumonia after being caught in a snowstorm in Northern China. Not the professor's fault. The government sent them there during some sort of research assignment. All very sad, and all part of the reasons he wants to defect."

My phone rang, interrupting us.

"Oh—What now?" Both of us said the same thing, at the same time, in almost the same tone of voice. Smith grinned at me. "Jinx," he said.

I answered the phone. It was Major Jones with a request for a meeting with him having to do with one of his unit's assignments.

"We're in the middle of planning a mission of our own, right now. Yes Sir, we. Someone in my own line of business. We've been assigned to work together. Yes, Sir. John Smith…"

The Major asked that I hand the phone over to Smith. Smith just grinned again as he took the phone.

"Yes," said Smith into the phone. "John Smith—although probably not the one you're expecting. I respectfully ask to tag along with the boy. I might have some additional resources that can be put at your disposal. My assignment is to work with him on anything that comes up—until reassigned. It would be my pleasure, Sir. Would I be horribly off the mark if I were to guess this could possibly be a BBB matter? Yes, I am fully briefed on those types of incidents. I am on the American response team for those. No, they don't happen on this side of the pond very often. Yes, we will be right over, Sir. Looking forward to it…"

Smith handed me back the phone. "He hung up," he said. "We'd better scrounge a jeep, or should we take your motorcycle?"

"You comfortable with that?" I asked. "It would be faster than waiting on another jeep to come by."

"I used to own one myself," Smith replied. "If you have that attachment to mount on the back of the seat to accommodate a passenger, I should be fine."

"I opted for that when I bought the bike," I said. "Girls—"

"Enjoy it," he interrupted, a smile on his face as if he had fond memories of having girls riding with him on his own bike. "In that case, we'd best be off. Can't keep the Major waiting."

Without another word we hopped on my bike and sped off, across the base, to the Major's office.

The Major was alone in his office—which was odd. I've never been there when there were fewer than two junior officers and a secretary in attendance. When I introduced them, the Major and the old man shook hands. "Cromer," said the old man. I took it to be some sort of password. Jones shot the old man an appraising look, then he nodded as if to himself.

"I told you I wasn't the fellow you were expecting," Smith said. Jones invited us to sit. We took three chairs off to the side of the Major's desk and settled in for an intimate little powwow. "I wish I was. Everything would be easier all the way 'round. I take it you have some news of something that 'our mutual friend' might find right up his alley?"

"It started off with reports of people going missing—not many, and not close together, but eventually enough of them for police reports to begin being forwarded to our main office, back East. Can't fault the local police agencies—not the sort of thing that becomes noticeable until *all* the reports have been examined in aggregate."

"And not unless those reports were examined," ventured the old man cautiously, "by people with our 'unique' experiences with other, shall we say, *mysterious* circumstances?"

"Exactly so," replied the Major. "Sad to say, people go missing all the time, all over the world. Sometimes of their own free will, sometimes due to criminal activity, but sometimes-"

"No one can find a clue as to why," Smith said. "As if they simply vanished into thin air, or something to the same effect."

"On the nose," said Major Jones. "*We* might be able to read a putative clew to better effect than the Yanks—present company excepted, of course..."

"Of course, of course, no offence taken," replied Smith. The old man sat back in his chair with a calculating look on his face, and a slight frown.

"You said that's how this incident 'started,' Major Jones?" I leaned forward in my own chair. "That seems to imply there were further developments of some other kind in the areas where the missing persons were reported. I'd guess that these other developments were close enough in time to make them seem connected to the disappearances, but not to a 'casual' observer?"

"Bright lad," said the Major. "When the only tool at hand is a hammer, every problem one is presented with begins to look like a nail. But if one is in possession of an entire toolbox, other possibilities may present themselves."

"Let me guess," said the old man. "Lights in the sky? Unexplained noises for which no one could locate a *reasonable* cause? Encounters with unusual wildlife that couldn't be ascribed to their witnesses being overfond of hard liquor? That sort of thing?"

"Ten out of ten, Professor Smith," said the Major. "Or as close as makes no difference. The only things you left out are ghosts, mysterious deaths of cattle, and new rumours of places giving rise to feelings of unease—if not outright paranoia on the part of those reporting the same."

"All hallmarks of BBB incidents," said the old man. "At least, according to reports I've been issued to study. Almost typical, I'd say. Yes, I think there is somewhat of 'our mutual friend's' nature in everything you've described. But I *think* you may be taking the long way round to get to what our actual—*trigger*, for want of a better word, to being called in for this little puzzle. Am I close?"

"Indeed," replied the Major. "We seem to have been given something 'out of the ordinary' with this most recent report."

"Which is?" I asked.

"A fortnight ago," began Major Jones, "a geologist and amateur archeologist wandered out of the region *somewhat* nearby to the Chaco Canyon Indian ruins. Not inside the National Park itself, mind you, but relatively close to it. He was suffering from a fever, raving a bit, and was hospitalized briefly. The attending physician wrote down the man's fever dreams and sent them on to someone who sent them to us. He'd found something extraordinary.

Something that bears looking into, at least by our little group."

"What did he find?" I asked.

"A pyramid…" said Major Jones. "One with a door that he couldn't open, and an inscription he couldn't read, but what brought it to the forefront of my superiors' curiosity was that it was built from a mineral the geologist could not identify. Now this man is highly respected in his field. His name is on some of the subject's standard textbooks. I was told, 'if this was a rock *this* man couldn't identify, then it must be something no one has ever seen before.'"

"What in the world?" I asked.

Smith looked at me sharply, looked back at Major Jones, then spoke. "Maybe nothing from *this* world," he said, frowning. "What happened to the geologist?"

"Recovered," said Jones. "Discharged from Hospital, returned to his home at the university where he worked— then vanished into thin air from a locked house—two days after he returned home. No one has seen hide nor hair of him since."

"That's weird," I said.

"Kid, you just said a mouthful," replied Smith. After that, the old man's face looked thoughtful and he got spooky quiet.

"We're putting together a team to go look at this pyramid," said the Major, after a long moment.

"I want in," said myself and the old man, almost with the same voice—like we were twins, or something.

"Get your gear together and report in the morning to the cargo helicopter I'm about to go to the Base Commander and requisition. I already have my lads packing their own kits. I'm loathe to bring any of the Yanks' regular soldiers into this, but I may need more manpower."

"Check the Stockade," I said. "The Commander might have a few hardcases in lockup he wouldn't mind being shed of for a few weeks."

"Excellent suggestion," said the old man.

Major Jones just nodded, as if that idea had already occurred to him.

"So, this place is next to a park?" I asked the old man once we got back to my quarters.

"Yeah," he replied. "Pueblo Indian ruins, discovered in the 1800s while it was still part of Mexico. FDR made it a park in 1901. Sandstone buildings, some pottery, irrigation ditches—lotsa Navajo Indians live in the area west of there. I remember reading about it in school. Best guess was that it was built sometime around the year 1000. After a long time, the weather got too dry for the Indians that lived there to survive, so they bugged out for someplace with more rain. Been deserted ever since. That's about all I know."

"Knowing the Major, he's probably already got somebody detailed to check some archeology books out of a library," I said.

"Or see if there's someone here on the base that studied archeology before they enlisted," said Smith. "Wouldn't surprise me a bit. Military people come from all sorts of backgrounds."

"What was that crack you made about 'not from this world' back there?" I'd been wanting to ask that question for over an hour. Now seemed like a good time.

"That's a little above your pay grade, Kid," Smith replied with a grin. "Suffice it to say that this unit you're attached to is detailed to check out anything that might be from 'somewhere else.' Just in case flying saucers are real—even if nobody believes in 'em anyway. Wouldn't do to get caught with our pants down if we were wrong about all that 'swamp gas' stuff."

"That's just a bunch of movie crap," I said. "Ain't it?"

"Behooves us to check out any possibility," said the old man. "If we're wrong, it's just a little time and money wasted. If we're right? Best to find out on the QT, before the Reds can cut a deal with some little green men." He laughed. "That'd ruin your whole day, right there. Probably nothin', but best to keep an open mind in case it ain't."

"So this 'BBB' stuff isn't the Better Business Bureau, I take it?" I asked.

"Just something we use," Smith replied, "to let each other know there's something out of the ordinary about some situation or other," said Smith. "Just a string of letters, a code phrase, nothing more. Got started back in the '40s or '50s, over in England. A bunch of guys kept showing up, right in the thick of it, when something weird went on. All of 'em went by the name 'John Smith.' Obviously a code name, and obviously workin' for some alphabet agency, but we never found out which agency. Thing is, every time they showed up, whatever happened got classified so Top Secret that *nobody* could dig it out of a file somewhere. Real *'Burn Before Reading'* crap. I doubt if even the Major has a high enough clearance to find out more than a tiny bit of it."

"Sounds spooky, and I used to work for the spooks," I said as I shoved the rest of my gear into my duffle.

"You and me both, Kid," said Smith. "You and me both. It's getting' dark. We better head over to the chow hall and grab a bite. Then make it an early night. I got a phone call to make about getting us some transport over to the helicopter when we wake up. I might have to call in a couple of favors from an old friend. Don't ask," he added as I started to open my mouth to do just that. "Let's just say I've got a few connections, and leave it at that, OK?"

"Yes Sir," I answered. "But I want to stop at the PX on the way back from chow and pick up a bottle of bourbon, or something. Something to get us to sleep faster."

"Now, *that* sounds like a plan!" The old man grinned.

Next morning, the old man had breakfast waiting for me when I got up. Evidently, he'd gone over to the chow hall while I was in the shower and picked us up a few things. My percolator was filling my quarters with the smell of fresh, strong coffee. There was a plate of ham and eggs and biscuits on the table waiting for me, and the old man had washed up the plate he must have used for his own meal. A couple of lunch boxes I'd never seen before were on the counter next to the stove. Smith was nowhere to be seen, but neither were my duffle and gear, or his gear bag. I sat down to eat—everything was still hot. When I'd poured my coffee, before I sat down, I'd noticed my oven was warm, so the warm plate of food was no mystery. As I was finishing up, he came back in. He was wearing a set of khaki fatigues and a floppy-brimmed boonie hat that looked as if he'd had them since Korea. The lack of stripes or pins made him look every inch an old archeologist who'd been out in the ass-end of nowhere often enough to have learned what gear was best for expeditions.

"We've got plenty of time to get to the airfield," he said. "Finish up. I'll wash your plate while you go take a whiz and make sure you haven't forgotten to pack something. I've got our gear loaded in my truck. I cleared it with the Major for us to take m'truck with the other cargo. We'll need it, and the Major is including a couple of jeeps, too."

"Thanks," I said. "Thanks for breakfast too. You packed us a lunch?"

"I never trust the in-flight catering supplied by an Army base," he replied with one of those quick grins I'd gotten used to seeing. "Something I learned from a British girl I used to know. She called it a Plowman's Lunch—a piece of fruit, some ham, a slice of sharp cheese, Branston relish, a couple of pickled onions, a hunk of French bread, and I scored us a thermos of cold buttermilk apiece, too. I'd have included a couple of bottles of Guinness, but I don't know if the Major would have approved."

"How did you wrangle that?" I asked, cleaning the last egg and bacon off of my plate with my last bite of biscuit.

"Traded the Chief of the Mess Hall a quart of Irish Whiskey for most of it," he said. "Requisitioned the rest from my contacts who delivered my truck to the base. I also got us some special gear that ain't exactly US Army issue. If we don't need it, it'll stay in the crate. If we do need it, we'll be damn glad to have it. But mum's the word unless we have to open that crate."

"You found a way to get on the Chief's good side?" I asked—disbelief loud in my voice.

"Bobby is a good guy," Smith said. "Just gotta get to know him. By the by, he thinks the Tullamore Dew came from you. All I did was lose a few hands of Bridge to him last night after you sacked out."

"Bobby?" I asked.

"Kid," Smith replied, "first thing you ever do, when you wind up on a base or a ship, is find out who the local Fixer is. The one who does swaps and deals to get ahold of stuff that ain't always on the inventory. Sometimes it's a Clerk, or a Motor Pool chief, a CPO, or even a cook, but there's always one somewhere. Get in good with them and you're set."

"I'll keep that in mind," I said.

"Gimme that plate, then go drain your bladder. I'll do KP while you're busy. Then we gotta haul ass to the helicopter. Major Jones won't like it if we're not loaded and ready when he gets there."

"Yessir," I said, standing up and heading for the toilet.

When I got outside, after taking care of the necessary, Smith had his truck cranked up and purring.

"That's a Studebaker!" I said in disbelief.

"Indeed it is," Smith replied, with pride in his voice. "1960 5E Transtar, three-quarter ton. I got the 4-wheel drive kit on her when I bought her new. Don't look like much now, but she's packin' a few surprises. She's tricked out with heavy-duty suspension, off-road no-flat tires, bigger gas tank, and a turbo-charged small-block 400 V8 instead of the original straight-6…"

It looked like a beat-up old farm truck. Faded red paint job—aged to an almost gun-metal gray, dented left-rear fender—and then the penny dropped. This thing was in disguise! Looked like an old beater, but probably ran like a racecar. The old man was showing me stuff about keeping a low profile that I'd never learn from the spooks in DC.

"Color me impressed," I said. "But if you can manage to keep it from going airborne while we get to the copter?"

"Piece of cake," said the old man. "Get in. Let's haul ass."

We got in. Ass was *impressively* hauled.

"I got to get me somethin' like this," I said as we pulled up near the cargo ramp of the Major's copter…

I should have expected there to be a problem with the Loadmaster for the copter. He didn't want to allow the old man's pick-up truck loaded in for the flight. Truth to tell, he wasn't keen on getting anything loaded quick enough for us to take off on time. It wasn't long before we were all standing there waiting on this desk-jockey to finish strutting around like a barnyard rooster, givin' Major Jones a hard time over what we needed loaded and secured for takeoff. I could tell the Major was getting angry. His Staff Sergeants both looked like they wanted to frogmarch Bantam Bob off someplace quiet for a little instruction in inter-services amity.

The old man and I had everything strapped down in the truck bed, plus a tarp secured over our gear, too. I looked up from tightening the last strap on the tarp to see Smith walking over to the Major. They had a little pow-wow of their own for just a second, then the Major did a polite little bow and sweep of one hand as if to tell Smith he had permission to cut in on this little dance routine. Smith saluted, then took three steps toward the Loadmaster.

Next thing I know, the rooster-boy was on his back on the ground and Smith was sitting on his chest, using his knees to keep our problem child's arms pinned to the runway. Smith had a switchblade knife about touching the Loadmaster's left eyeball. The old man's whisper was just barely loud enough for me to hear.

"What we have here," Smith was saying, "is a failure to communicate. Now, I have enough rank to get away with anything I choose to do to you, little boy. The way I see it, you have two choices—you can either get this bird loaded up and certified ready to lift—pronto, or you can expect a long hospital stay, a court martial an' dishonorable discharge, followed by a chance to set yourself up with a white cane, tin-cup, and pencil business after make you eat *both* your eyeballs. Notice how no one is pulling me off of you and threatening *me* with charges? That's because I outrank the Base Commander—and almost anyone else that ain't sittin' a desk in DC right this minute. So, unless you suddenly outrank the Deputy Director of the C fuckin' I A, you're gonna dismount your damned high horse and get this bird loaded—or I'm gonna make a bloody mess of your face *right now. Capiche?*"

Fifteen minutes later, the truck, two jeeps, the Major's Royal Marines, and what I presume were the guys the Major "borrowed" from the stockade were on the helicopter, taking off for New Mexico. Smith was huddled up with a couple of the Royal Marines, and Major Jones was giving him a look like Smith was being reappraised in the Major's opinions.

"You going to get in trouble for that?" I asked Smith when we had a moment in private.

"Not unless that little shit is dumber than he looks. If he presses charges, it'll blow up in his face. He was being insubordinate to Major Jones—to begin with. He was delaying a UN sanctioned operation involving US, UK, Canadian, *and* European NATO forces, not to mention the people who give *me* orders—I've got to wonder how many times he's pulled this little prima donna crap in the past. The General might just want to be shed of him, anyway. If he's got a record of pulling stunts like this, he could find himself mustered out, or transferred to a one-man weather station in Antarctica."

"What was that trick you used to throw him to the ground?" I'd been itching to ask that question.

"You already know it," Smith said. "You learned it in Basic Training. A judo throw—you just haven't been alive long enough to practice it as long as me, that's all."

"You play rough, Old Man," I said.

"You do too," he replied. "When you're forced to. In our business, sometimes you have to do stuff that gives you nightmares later. But at least you're alive to *have* nightmares."

I thought about Jamaica, and Berlin, and had to admit he was right. We didn't talk much the rest of the flight. He got a far-away look on his face—as if he were remembering the causes of his *own* nightmares. After a while, he grunted and pulled the brim of his boonie hat down over his eyes. I don't know if he took a nap, or was just avoiding conversation. After a few minutes, I got up and wandered forward to snag a cup of coffee from the Sergeant-Major. It burned going down. I think it had something stronger than just coffee beans in it. I was glad of it, too.

The other British Sergeant was having a little chat with the conscripted troops from the base stockade. They were passing around a very non-regulation bottle, and a pack of smokes. I couldn't make out what they were talking about, but the occasional laugh and knee-slap told me he was getting through to them.

"Good man," I heard the Major say behind me. I didn't hear him sneak up on me over the roar of the copter's engines. I shot him a quick glance—just long enough to see he was meaning his Sergeant. "Here's hoping he won't have to waste time convincing them to accept his authority, once we reach the landing zone."

"Looks good so far," I said. "He's not someone you want to be on the bad side of, for sure."

"Loyalty is a two-way street," said Major Jones. "Convince a man you'll have his back through thick and thin, and they'll usually repay the respect. Convince them you respect *them*, and the job practically finishes itself. Those could be outstanding soldiers—I suspect that someone failed to earn their respect before demanding theirs."

"That's how it usually goes," I replied. "When you grow up not being able to trust anyone but yourself, it's hard to believe it when you finally find someone you *can* trust. The army is full of guys like that. Could have gone a lot further than the stockade if only…"

"'*If only*' is what my men are all about," replied the Major. "Now—go relax, yourself. It may not be long before someone is shooting at us—again…" He laughed.

"Story of my life," I sighed. Then I went back to see if I could join in with the Sergeant and his new best friends…

"Captain Darby," said the Staff Sergeant as I shuffled over. I don't think I'll ever get used to being a passenger in any aircraft I could walk around in. Felt kind of funny not to be in the pilot's seat. Sure, I'd *trained* to fly a copter, but I wasn't any kind of expert.

"Sergeant," I said by way of an ice-breaker, "gentlemen. How are we doin'?"

"We seem to be making progress," he said. "I'll wager that the lads will give a good accounting of themselves, if need be."

"Good," I said, "good—might be nothing to this, but if there is, best to be prepared. This building is close enough to the park that it might be just another part of that site. One nobody ever saw before, sure, but just another old relic."

"Seen a few of those in my time," said the Sergeant. "I remember one castle in Germany that reports said was haunted. We got there and it was just a Dark Ages pile of rubble the locals had been afraid to go near for 400 years or more. Turned out there was a serial killer in the area— back in the day. The story passed through so many generations, it had turned into a local legend. They swore that the killer was still active. Even though there weren't any records of mysterious deaths for centuries before we arrived. Just old wives' tales."

"Sounds about right," I said. "I've been to haunted houses before, back home in Virginia. Just old houses about to fall apart, but they *looked* spooky enough to be a horror movie set." I laughed. Then I looked at the new boys and asked the Sergeant to introduce them.

"Brock Peterson," said the Sergeant, indicating the man nearest him. "The Private scored Marksman with rifle and pistol, but if there is a betting pool in his unit, he's the one holding the book. Next to him is Corporal Joe Tasker, a farmboy from your neck of the woods. Private Ainslee is next to him, then Privates Parker, Bowles, Sanders, Johanson, Smith, Raintree, Harper, Brooks, Maxies, Louder, Meadows, Ayres, and Sergeant Beckett over there on the end. I wasn't informed why they were in the Stockade. But I believe it's safe to say that they may have a tiny little problem with authority, officially. My opinion is that they have never been assigned to an officer who earned their respect—speakin' as someone who's spent some time in the lock-up a time or three, m'self."

I had to smile. The Major was right. Show a man respect and he'll most likely return it. "Gentlemen," I said. "Pleasure to be working with you. You'll find that this isn't your normal unit. The Major will expect you to follow orders, but improvise when orders don't cover every situation. He won't be sending you into danger, so much as out in front of you, leading the way. This group generally has two sorts of missions, right Sergeant?"

"Too right," said the Sergeant. "Either it's a bloody cakewalk, or someone is trying to send as many of us home in a body bag as possible. The cakewalks are boring, but safe. The 'walking into a hornet's nest' is something else again. Stay alert, use your eyes and ears, and don't take stupid chances if the shit hits the fan, as you Yanks say. Captain?"

"I'm Captain Darby," I said. "I'm a pilot. Usually, I'd be up front flying the bus, but choppers aren't my bag. I flew Saber jets in Korea, then got shanghaied into working with a bunch of alphabet agencies on the ground, then recruited into joining the Major's unit because I have a knack for coming home alive. I'm telling you this because if I spot an ambush and holler 'Get DOWN' I'm gonna be halfway to the ground with my trench knife out to dig myself a foxhole to hide in before *you* hear the words leave my mouth. I don't give a *damn* what you did to wind up in the stockade. I. Don't. Care. You're with *us* now, and that means we want to get you home safely—which means that if the Staff Sergeants, myself, or the Major give you an order, not listening can earn you a pine box to go home in. One last thing, the old man—"

"Yeah," interrupted Private Bowles. "I saw him whip the Load Master's ass and nobody said a word to him about it. Who the hell is he?"

"His name," I said. "Is *'Doctor Smith.'* He's a certified badass, and I saw him give orders to a couple of Generals. I don't know what his rank is, or even if he has a military rank, but I trust him. I'd say, follow any order or suggestion he might give you as if he were God, Himself. I've never met anyone like him. He's smart, experienced, and he has skills I wouldn't even *begin* to know how to learn. My best guess is that he's some kind of retired spy—so don't go messing with his truck, the crates in it, or worse yet, *him.* That might turn out to be all kinds of bad. And—he's standing right behind me, isn't he?"

"Not bad, Kid," Smith said as he patted my shoulder and walked around to stand beside me. "OK, listen up badasses," he added, addressing the young soldiers. "You don't know me from Adam's off ox. If you know what's good for you, you'll forget I even exist after this little job is finished. I get called out to do tricky shit, and I manage to get the job done and go home again. It's a dirty job. But it's mine and I'm damned good at it. If you hear Captain Darby yell for you to get down because we walked into an ambush, rest assured I'll already have my foxhole dug and be shootin' at the ambushers before he can open his mouth. Yeah, I'm old. That just means I'm so good that nobody has been able to kill me yet. Not *quite* somethin' I'm likely to want to brag about. I've been through some *shit,* Boys. None of it was fun. None of it was glamorous. All of it was necessary for the security of our great country. This little party we're on promises to be simple—so keep your eyes open! I don't trust simple. That's the kind of thing that turns sour when you least expect it."

"Just what are we up against?" I asked.

"All I know," said the old man, "is that close to this park we're going to, there is a building that no one ever saw until recently. Wrong style architecture for the area, should have been found before now—it's out of place. This unit was founded and chartered to investigate out of place objects. Sometimes it's nothin', sometimes it's somethin' you won't be allowed to talk about later—and sometimes, whatever it is doesn't want to be investigated. If we're lucky, it'll turn out to be just a pile of rocks that everybody managed to overlook before."

"And if we're unlucky?" Sergeant Beckett asked.

"That's why you boys got railroaded into this," the old man replied. You are the insurance policy, so to speak. You and the British squads will have to work together, so don't cause trouble. They've got experience with things that could '*object*' to being investigated. Watch and learn. Follow orders. Don't wander off. You do that, and I'll see that your records are cleared. Do this right, and you *might* just be asked to transfer to this unit full time—which means a raise in pay and possible promotions, as well as a little bonus to go with your honorable discharge when your enlistment is up. Y'all up for that?"

They looked at one another, then at Beckett. "I believe I can speak for the rest of the men when I say 'yes,' Sir.

Sounds like our kind of trouble. And the thing about trouble? It's never boring." He grinned. "We're in."

"Good lads," said the old man. "Smoke 'em if you got 'em, finish your drinks, then try and catch some sleep. I'm going back to my seat to finish my nap." He turned to me and said "you too, Captain. That's an order." Then he went back to his seat, pulled his hat down over his eyes, and got very still.

"You heard the man," said the Staff Sergeant. "Polish off what's in your hands and get some shut-eye. We may be running short on sleep once we hit the ground and find out what we're facing. Never miss a chance to eat, sleep, or hit the latrine. You never know when the next opportunity might arise." He looked at me. "Captain, with all due respect, you have your orders. I respectfully advise you to follow 'em."

"Yes sir, Sergeant Devon," I said. "Excellent advice. I shall do that very thing, right now." We grinned at each other, and I went to my seat to attempt to get some sleep.

We landed shortly after dawn. Within an hour or two, we'd unloaded the helicopter and set ourselves up a base camp. The major had a tent he shared with Lieutenant Anderson and Sergeant-Major Beckett. Sergeant-Major Heath and the troops shared a larger tent, big enough for all of them, and the copter crew had another tent that was attached to a slightly larger, but fully functional, mess tent. The cook was one of the helicopter crew. His gear had been stashed in the copter before the rest of us got loaded in. I think he kept a lot of his gear on the copter all the time, in fact. Saved time and aggravation on the load-in, anyway. The old man and I had a smaller tent—just to ourselves. For a quickly set-up camp, the boys did a good job.

After a quick breakfast of some pretty damn good Army chow, most of us set out in the old man's truck and the two jeeps for the spot on the map where our target should be located. The flight crew, the Major's Aide-De Camp, and a pair of the Privates stayed behind to guard the camp and set up a latrine. All three vehicles were a bit overloaded, but we managed to make it work. We were moving slowly—what with there being no real road to speak of. I'd seen old logging roads back home that'd make this glorified game trail look like a major highway. The boys took turns dismounting and quick-marching alongside and behind the jeeps, then hopping up to trade places with another squad. We did have to detour around a couple of little ravines, but that didn't waste too much time. Finally, our little parade rolled up to a wide clearing on the trail. We were close to the map coordinates of the building we'd come to investigate. We couldn't see it yet, but we had to be close.

The Major and the old man put their heads together for a few minutes, then we split up to perform a search. The Sergeants each took a squad, as did the Major, and headed out. The old man and I took the pair of Privates from the squad that had been split between our search crew and the base camp. After about half an hour, we found our mysterious building. The old man radioed back to the Major and the Sergeants that we'd found the thing. While we waited for them to catch up, the four of us examined the pile of rocks we'd come all this way to see.

It was a pyramid, four-sided, roughly eighteen feet on each side, and about twenty-five feet tall. The rocks it was built out of didn't match any of the local rock we'd seen so far—either on the trail or near the camp. There wasn't any visible door, but there was what *looked like* the outlines of a door. The top didn't come to a peak, like an Egyptian pyramid. Instead, it looked like it was flat, about four square feet, but we couldn't see the roof of it to tell for sure.

The rock looked like melted granite—or some kind of dirty-gray quartz—and was slick to the touch. There wasn't any mortar between the stones. The edges of each stone were rounded where they joined together. Looked like photos I'd seen of ruins in South America, to tell the truth. Each stone was roughly twice the size of a normal concrete block—thirty inches or so by sixteen inches tall. It looked old. I mean really old—like, when dinosaurs ruled the Earth-old. There wasn't any weathering, though. It raised the hairs on the back of my neck just to stand near it. The old man took a couple of tools out of his pockets and started tapping and scratching the surface of one wall. He grunted, then tried to chip off a little chunk of the rock.

"I can't even scratch it," he said. "Tom, get your compass out and walk all the way around it."

I did, and about halfway around, I understood why he'd asked me to try. "It's magnetic," I said. "It drags the South end of my compass needle to it, no matter where I stand. But, it's pretty weak."

"Let me try something," said the old man. He pulled a rock-hound's hammer out of his pack, and smacked the hell out of one of the rocks about eyeball height.

The rock made a faint ringing sound—like a Buddhist Temple bell being rung—but very faint. I'd expected it to sound like a rock being smacked with a hammer. I'd expected wrong, I guess.

"Look at this," said the old man. He showed me the pointed end of the hammer. Or, at least what used to be the pointed end.

"It's bent," I said. "Blunted, but that can't be right. What kind of rock can blunt a hammer?"

"I don't believe it," said the old man. "I see it with my own eyes, but I just can't make myself believe it. I can't scratch it, I can't knock a chip off of it, and I just ruined the pick-end of my hammer trying. It just can't be—but it acts like it is."

"Is what?" I asked.

"If I didn't know it was impossible," said the old man. "I'd swear this rock was a diamond. Can't be, though. It just can't be."

"I didn't know they made diamonds *this* big," I replied.

"That's why it's impossible," he said. "Nature *doesn't*. If these bricks were really diamonds, they'd have to be *manufactured*. Nobody I've ever heard of can make an artificial diamond as big as these bricks—much less, enough of them to build *this* thing…"

Just about then, the rest of our crew showed up. The old man went over to have another little talk with the Major. When they finished their chat, the Major started giving orders to his Sergeants. When he was done, he walked over to me.

"No visible entry," he said. "That leaves two possibilities—a tunnel from underneath, or an entry on the roof." He looked around at the spindly little trees, few and far between, as well as looking like they'd been the victims of a drought that'd lasted for decades. "Nothing here to use as supports for a tunnel, so I won't risk men digging underneath this—*mystery*. We didn't bring any ladders, so we'll have to improvise if we're going to get a look at the roof."

Sergeant-Major Heath began calling out instructions. "I want a rope thrown over the top, and down the opposite side. Sergeant Pitts, take your squads to the opposite side and deploy them to anchor the rope. Sergeant Devon, I want your best climber to scale this side and reccy the roof."

"Yas, SIR," shouted the Sergeants.

"Parker, front and center," said Sergeant Devon.

"Reporting, Sir," replied Private Parker as he ran up.

"Parker," said Devon. "You're the smallest and lightest we have. Think you can climb a rope?"

"Absolutely Sir," Parker said. "Piece of cake."

"Good lad," said Devon.

"Ready on this side," called Sergeant Pitts.

"Off you go, then," said Devon to Parker. Parker pulled a pair of leather gloves from his hip pocket, pulled them on, and proceeded to shimmy up the rope like a circus acrobat.

"Good man, that," observed the Major. "Make a fine addition to our unit."

Parker reached the top, threw his left leg over, and rolled out of sight onto the roof. A moment later, he stood up and shouted down. "There's a plate set into the stone up here. Like a manhole cover, but shiny as a mirror. I've got room to walk all the way 'round it without setting foot on it." He kneeled down and touched what we guessed to be the 'manhole cover.'

"It's cold as ice," he shouted. "Slick as ice, too. No handle on it, and no hole to put a crowbar through to lift it. No hinges, either. Should I stand on it and see if it gives any?"

"If it looks safe to you," shouted the Major, "then try it."

Parker stood upright, gingerly put one foot, then the other on his find, then shouted back. "It doesn't seem to give any because of my weight," he said. Then he screamed like a damned soul being taken straight to Hell.

A light like a camera flash blinded me for an instant. Parker's voice cut off in mid scream. When I could see again, Parker was gone, and the rope he used to climb up slithered down the sides of the pyramid as if it had been cut in the middle.

"Pull back!" Major Jones shouted. "Rifles at the ready!"

The old man had both Colts out and their hammers back. Major Jones drew his Webley and cocked its hammer. In his left hand he held a peculiar-looking grenade, ready to arm and throw. I had my own Colt out and at the ready. All the soldiers had their rifles pointed at the building. Pitts and Devon had their tommy guns unslung from their shoulders and were racking the slides. We waited…

Nothing happened. We waited…

"Stand down, but stay alert!" Major Jones ordered. "Report!"

"Rope was cut straight through," Sergeant Pitts called back. "Like someone sliced it with a cut-throat razor!"

"Same on this side," reported Sergeant Devon. "Cut clean through—not a fiber out of place on the end!"

"Well, *shit*," said the old man.

"Heath, front and center," said Major Jones.

"SIR, yes Sir," said the Sergeant-Major as he ran over to the Major and snapped off a salute.

"Take one of our squads, plus a squad of the Yanks, and form up a perimeter fifteen yards out from the building. Two-man teams, one of ours and one of the Yanks. Stay in sight of one another. Weapons ready and safeties locked. You're in charge. Keep them out of harm's way if at all possible. Do not, under any circumstances, approach the building. You keep one jeep here. You'll have to go get it and navigate to whatever high ground seems sufficient. That will be your camp. Professor Smith?"

"Here Sir," the old man replied. "I've got a little weather balloon we can anchor to a stake in the ground in case we need a navigation marker for the helicopter. I suggest we put it nearby, but not too close to the building."

"Good man," said the Major. "The rest of us, back to camp. I need the radio in the helicopter to report to Geneva. This just got serious…"

Everyone deployed as ordered. The teams left at the building looked both frightened and angry. I doubted if any of them would get any sleep much more than a wary doze when it was their turn off watch. As we left, I felt eyes on the back of my neck. Somehow, I couldn't convince myself that those eyes belonged to the men we left on guard. I felt like I was hiding from a sniper. I hadn't felt this way since Korea. Didn't much like it, either.

The old man drove his truck back to the base camp. Sergeant Pitts drove the other jeep back. Devon stayed with Sergeant-Major Heath at the pyramid. It was late afternoon when we got back to camp. The old man went with the Major to the helicopter. I went back to our tent and checked my gear. Eventually, I got hungry and wandered over to the Mess Tent. I don't remember what I ate. Nobody talked much that night. The old man wasn't back yet when I finally sacked out. He was up and getting dressed when I woke up the next morning.

"Shake a leg," he said. We've had a radio call from the troops at the building. Sounds like a cougar is stalking them. Lost two men who were on guard duty…"

"What? Who'd we lose?" I asked as I pulled my pants on and reached for a shirt.

"Didn't catch their names," said the old man. "One of the Brits and one of the new boys. I ran over here as soon as the Major started giving orders to move out—back to the building."

"I didn't realize that there were any wild cats in this area," I said as I started lacing up my boots. "We better load up the long guns."

"I got us a thermos of coffee and some breakfast in the truck" he said. "Stopped by the mess tent for a second. The cook put together what amounts to a sack lunch for everyone, too. Ours are in the truck with the breakfasts. The chopper crew are the only ones staying here—and they've got their machine guns out in case the thing heads this way once we start making noise up there. The cook even had his tommy gun leaned up where he could reach it quick. Haven't seen a cook armor up since the bad old days."

"Let me hit the latrine," I said. "I'll meet you at the truck in five."

"Ride in the back with the new boys," he said. "Sergeant-Major Beckett will be up front with me. He got antsy about the Major heading into the 'unknown' without him."

"Understood," I said as I reached our tent's flap. The old man was hitching his gun belt up as I left.

I hopped into the back of the old man's truck with half a dozen of the new guys. We nodded to each other, and Smith started up the truck. We rolled out of the camp at a pretty good clip. Yesterday's trip saw the guys clearing rocks out of the path, so we were able to make better time. No one spoke much as we bounced up the dirt track towards the building. Everyone just held their rifles tight and kept checking their ammo pouches, over and over again. I could smell the fear and anger coming off them— like soured sweat. They'd lost two friends to this mission already. But I could tell they'd drawn closer together, started to gel as a team, because of their shared pain. They were scanning the sides of the road as if they expected the big cat to leap out of the skimpy underbrush at any second. It was a real white-knuckle ride. Finally, we caught up to the Major's two jeeps and the British unit about the same time as we reached the clearing where the building sat.

Sergeant-Major Heath had his remaining men together there as we bailed out of our little convoy. Two blood-stained rolls of lumpy canvas marked where the bodies of our dead friends had been retrieved and covered. The Major looked angrier than I'd ever seen him.

"Report," said the Major.

"The only thing we heard were their screams," said Heath. "No growls, no brush rattling, no *nothing!*"

"Anyone see the cat?" Major Jones asked.

"Not a sign," Heath replied. "Not even any paw-prints. Just our two boys ripped to pieces. It's like one of those 'panther on the moors' stories from back home, Sir. Our boys were slaughtered, and not so much as a whisper of what did it. I'm sorry sir, I had no suspicion of anything out of the ordinary until they'd been killed."

Our Boys, I thought. *Like he doesn't see any difference between the Brits and Americans on the team.* I looked around at the faces of the men. They'd caught it too. Heath got a lot more respect from the Americans right that moment. As horrible as the situation was, the team just got a whole lot tighter. Whatever the menace was, we'd be facing it *together* from now on. Not as a collection of American misfits and British Special Forces, but as one team, together. I nodded to myself. Glancing at Professor Smith, I saw that he was thinking along the same lines. The Major didn't show it, but I believe he'd had to have been blind not to pick up on the shift in tone of the group.

"All right men," he said. "Form up in squads, one senior in command, and however many as we have enough of the ranks to fill the squads out. Heath, Pitts, Beckett, Professor Smith, Darby—divvy up the men between you. I'll take three men myself and go examine the guard posts where our boys were killed. The rest of you, spiral out from the building and check everything. Look for footprints, animal fur caught on brush—anything. Do we have enough radios for each squad?"

"Absolutely, Sir!" Pitts said. "Enough for two radios per squad."

"Men," Beckett said. "Form up on the squad leaders. Stay close together. Keep your eyes and ears open. Sidearms are to be cocked and locked, with a round in the chamber ready to fire as soon as the safety is off. Those of you with machine guns, set for burst fire—not fully automatic—so as to keep better control of muzzle flip."

"Thirty minutes out, thirty minutes back," added the Major. "If you find the thing, kill it. Fire a flare so the rest of us can come running. I want this thing dead. Don't take chances. All right, move out."

"Raintree," I said to one of my own squad. "You're our radio man as well as flare gun man. Clip them out of the way, but where you can reach them in a hurry. Don't block your rifle sling, either. You may need it in a hurry. Bowles, Ashcroft, are you two checked out on those machine guns?"

The two men looked at one another, then nodded.

"I grew up in Chicago," Bowles said. "I know Tommies."

"Rated expert with this Sten," Ashcroft said in his British lilt. "A grease-gun is like part of me arm. Show me a target, Captain. I'll perforate it, right enough."

"Let's move out," I said.

We had just turned back to do the inner leg of our sweep when one of the other squads sent up their flare. I glanced at my squad; they'd zeroed in on the first sounds of gunfire that'd quickly followed the light from the flare.

"Crap," said Raintree as he slung his rifle and reached for the radio. "Double-time, Cap?" he asked.

"I hate running," I said. I don't remember drawing my Colt, but there it was in my hand. I holstered it. The radio crackled to life, but the message was unintelligible. "Let's haul ass, boys…"

"Sir," Ashcroft answered, then looked at Bowles. They nodded to each other and spread out a few extra steps between themselves. We started towards the flare at a dead run. I followed right behind Raintree as he paced Bowles and Ashcroft. Raintree had the radio in his off hand at first, then clipped it to his belt as we ran. Nothing but crackles of static coming out of it anyway.

Another flare went off. Same location, but we'd gotten closer by then. It was beginning to sound like a pitched battle up ahead. Some of the other squads must have been closer than us. Gotten there quicker, anyway.

"Careful, to the west," came the Major's voice over the radio. *"It headed that way. It's wounded…"*

"Darby's squad," said Raintree into the radio. "Coming up from the south. Should we angle west to pursue?" *Good man,* I thought.

"Roger that," said the Major. The static on the radio was almost drowning him out. *"We're following its trail now. Be careful—it killed two of our boys before we knew it was there."*

"Shit," said Bowles. "Now it's personal…" We all nodded in agreement.

We turned a hard left and started angling to the west.

Seemed like forever, but we met up with the Major and most of the rest of the team fairly quickly. No more flares had been sent up. No more gunfire, either. Longest twenty-minute dead-run I could remember, before we caught up with the team.

"Looked like a bear," said the Major to my unspoken question as I reached his side. "Moved like a bloody panther, though. Never did get a good view of it to be sure. Whatever this thing is, it's a killer. We'll have to recover the bodies as we go back to camp. Nothing we could do for them. DeAngelo looked like he'd lost a fight with a sawmill. Oscars—decapitated is the kindest way to put it. We hit it with concentrated fire from six machine guns. It just roared at us and ran away. Plenty of blood along its trail, though. We hurt it, but not enough…"

"How big?' I asked as I caught my breath. *Two of the best the Major has—had*, I thought. *Good men, gone…*

"Over two meters, standing upright," said the Major. "Damn near a meter across at the shoulder. Black as night. Smelled like a cesspit—even from as far away as *we* were when the shooting started. Ran on all fours when it escaped."

"Sounds like a bear all right," I said. "But even if it had rabies, I've never heard of a bear tearing a man's head off instead of biting a chunk out of 'em."

"It'll be even more dangerous now we've wounded it," said Sergeant-Major Beckett.

"Indeed," replied the Major.

I looked around for the old man. Professor Smith was across the clearing, looking at a bush. I saw him pick something off of it, shake his hand like he'd been stung, then he turned and walked over to us.

"Damnedest fur I've ever seen," he said as he reached us. "I'm no zoologist, but I've never seen anything like this. Feels like spun *glass*, not *hair*. Cut my thumb trying to pick it off that bush." He put the bit of fur in an envelope, then tucked the envelope away in a pocket of his jacket. "Damned bush didn't have thorns, so it had to be the fur that cut me. Plus, it walked away from enough firepower to win the Battle of the Bulge. We *hit* it, and hit it *hard!* Damned thing *ought* to be a bloody heap of guts, but *it ran off!*"

"We're losing the light," said Beckett. "Time to head back to camp, I suggest. Not wanting to face that *thing* in the dark. We can pick up our casualties on the way back."

"My thoughts exactly," said the Major. "Just once, I'd like to meet a bugger that wasn't immune to bullets…"

What? I thought.

"Back to camp," said the Major. "Devon, Pitts, your squads are rear-guard. Look alive, men. Back to the helicopter. We'll look for this thing's trail at first light."

"We'll open the crate of special gear I brought in my truck," said the old man as I fell in beside him. "We're gonna need some bigger guns for this thing."

"Got a bazooka in that crate?" I asked.

"Close," he answered. "But no cigar…" I couldn't get a word out of him the rest of the way back to camp. When we reached the site where our friends had been killed, the Major ordered that a pair of kludged-up sledges be made to put their bodies on, wrapped in ponchos since we didn't have any tarps to cover them with. The men traded off dragging their comrades back to camp. Anger lent them strength. In all my years of service, I don't remember seeing a unit that was more pissed-off than we were that evening. We ate something, don't remember what, then posted guards and the rest of us went silently to our tents to sleep.

I almost felt sorry for the beast. Almost... When we finally caught up with it, it was gonna die an ugly death. *Sonovabitch must pay,* I thought as a fitful sleep finally took me.

"Go get yourself some breakfast," said the old man as I clawed my way to awareness. I'd made a run to the latrine, half sleepwalking, just as the sun was clearing the horizon. He was opening his crate of special gear that had been in the back of his truck all along. I saw stuff that looked like flame throwers or bazookas, wrapped up in the crate. "Go eat," he said. "You won't be any good without enough fuel to do the necessary."

"I need coffee, and answers," I said.

"The cook has the coffee, and food," the old man replied. "I'll have all the answers you're likely to get—afterwards."

"That thing," I said, stubbornness getting the better of me. "I want it dead."

"We all do," the old man replied. "In due time, we'll kill it—I hope."

"Hope?" I asked, rubbing sleep out of my eyes.

"If it's a wild animal," he said. "We can kill it if we find it. If it came out of that pyramid, then it isn't *just* an animal."

"What?" I asked.

"Go the fuck and eat something, and guzzle as much coffee as you can stomach. I need you awake and alert, boy! This thing needs killing. You aren't gonna be any use hungry and half asleep. Go! Eat. We got a monster to hunt…"

I looked at him, really looked, as if for the first time. He was a frail old man, but he looked like Superman's pissed-off grandpa right then. I went to grab me some food and coffee without any further argument.

When I came back, the Major was there at the old man's truck, reaching into the crate Smith had opened, touching whatever was inside. He looked at the old man, who nodded as if giving permission to the Major's unspoken question. The Major pulled out a short, oddly fat-looking rifle. It had a skeletal-sort of stock made of wood and metal, with a thick shoulder pad, some sort of short scope for a sight, and a thick barrel that couldn't have been twenty-five inches long.

"What is it?" I asked.

Smith looked at me and then at the Major. "Something experimental," he said. The Major nodded, hefted the heavy-looking thing to his shoulder in a marksman's stance, and sighted through the little tube.

"It's a peep sight," said the Major after a moment's glance through the tube. "Not a scope at all. No lenses—just a crosshair. I'm guessing the range must be rather like a shotgun."

"One-hundred-yard maximum range," said Smith. "For now, anyway. But the rounds for it pack the punch of a hand grenade. These five in this crate are all that exist outside of the lab that developed it. Drum magazine fed, five round magazines, semi-automatic. Only two magazines per rifle, I'm afraid. We'll have to assign these to your best marksmen. We've no extra rounds to practice with, so every shot *must* count. The thing shrugged off everything we fired at it so far. I'm betting, and the Powers That Be back me up on this, the creature won't be shrugging *these* off!"

"What's in the other crate?" Major Jones asked.

"Body armor," said the old man. "Some oddball thing the lab dreamed up. Light as a pair of cotton coveralls, flexible as silk, but stiffens up like sheet steel if it suffers an impact. Some weird lab effect of 'super-fluid dynamics' is what the lab-rats said. I don't understand it, myself. There are twenty suits in that crate, with face masks, gloves, and little booties to go over standard-issue combat boots. Damned things cost as much as *two* Sherman tanks, *each!* We'll look like Martians from some '50s drive-in movie, but with these, we won't lose any more men to this critter. At least, not from friendly fire. I'd have gotten them out before, but they're so far above Top Secret that I'd have been risking a firing squad if I had."

"The Home Office will be hearing from me in my reports about *that*," said Major Jones. "Bloody *paperwork* cost me the lives of some of my best men! I don't hold you to any blame, Professor, but still…"

"I had to see this creature with my own eyes," Smith replied. "I had to know it actually *existed*. The hope was that the building would turn out to be something ordinary, abandoned, some relic of the past. If it wasn't, this was the best hope we were given—these guns and armor. I had to see the threat with my own eyes. See what it could do. See that we actually *needed* this gear before I could admit that I had it with me. Until then, *my* hands were tied, too." The disgust in his voice could cut diamonds. "Wouldn't be the first time a pile of red tape killed more people than it protected. Won't be the last time, either. Mark my words, our own bureaucrats will always put their *careers* above the safety of our boys in uniform. They're worse than any enemy soldiers I've ever faced. Damned fools…"

"Agreed, Professor," said Jones. "But ours is not to question why—"

"Major," replied Smith. "I shan't argue with you. Now, let's get these suits and guns to as many of our boys as we can, and set the camp up to defend itself while we go kill that thing. Nobody without a suit can go with us. These guns are too dangerous. By the way, your field kits wouldn't happen to include any flamethrowers, would it?"

"No," said the Major. "More's the pity. Still, I wager the lads could rig up a few little toys of their own. I'll put my Sergeants-Major on that little task."

"Good lad," replied Smith. "See that you do."

Half an hour later, we were suited up. The old man was right; the armor did make us look like extras from some cheesy old monster movie.

"Professor?" asked the Major. Tell the men about this special equipment, please. We'll discuss tactics once we know what we have to work with."

"Thank you, Major Jones," said the old man. He raised his voice a bit to address the men. "Boys! Listen up!' Smith said. "These monkey suits are to protect you from the back-blast from the explosives these rifles spit out. Light one off too close to yourselves, and the suits absorb the concussion as well as protect you from shrapnel. They're proof against anything short of a howitzer shell to the face, more or less. Or a flamethrower, or napalm—they'll burn just like any cloth if it gets hot enough. You five with the rifles. You have ten, and only ten, rounds each. Two drum magazines each. That's *it*. There aren't any more any closer than Fort Knox. Don't waste a shot. The sight works like the peep sight on your standard-issue rifles. But whatever you put the crosshairs on is going to go boom. The rounds are two inches in diameter. Penetration is crap. They're not meant to punch a hole in something and blow up on the other side. When they hit something, they explode. They've got as much power as a hand grenade going off. Maximum range, and I do mean *maximum*, is one hundred yards. The best range is between fifteen and fifty yards. Anything closer than ten to fifteen yards, and you're going to wind up knocked flat on your ass by the blast, unable to move again until the suits un-armor themselves. The closer the blast, the longer you'll be locked up, rigid, and helpless while the thing runs at you—if you don't kill it straight off. The best way to use the rifles is to stand with one leg back, to prop you up when the blast wave reaches you. The suit will go rigid to protect you, but you have to be braced for the blast to keep from being knocked down. The closer the blast, the longer it takes for the suit to stop acting like sheet metal. Fifty yards off, you'll be free to move again in less than a second. Ten yards or less, you'll be a statue for five to ten seconds. Being a statue is a scary way to watch your enemy run up and tear your head off…"

"Best tactics?" Major Jones asked.

"The old-fashioned way," said the Professor. "Advance in a line abreast, the five new weapons scattered through the line, everyone without the new weapons try to keep the thing from dodging around while the rest line up a good shot. Hit the thing with everything we can, and hope we can kill it. If we can't, it'll kill us. All of us. The damn thing fights like an animal. But it hides and plans like a man. It's hunting us while we hunt it!"

"Can we booby-trap the building? The area around the building, I mean," asked the Major. "My Sergeants suggested using the few hand grenades we have with tripwires to pull the pins, spaced carefully around the clearing where the building sits."

"We can try that," said Smith. "But I think we need a distraction, too. We can't actually damage the building with anything we have on hand, but maybe we can make the thing *think* we can. Build a fire against the door-looking things? Put our tripwires where it can trip them if we can convince it to run up to the building?"

"*If* we can make it believe we have the means to break into the building," the Major replied.

"That's a big 'if,'" I said.

"It is, indeed," said the Major. "The lads have everything packed up, including a few surprises they were able to concoct. Shall we form up and move out?"

"Should we leave one of the riflemen with the new gear here to defend the camp?" I asked. "I'd hate for the thing to out-think us and attack the camp while we go off and lay traps for it."

"I've considered that," said the Major. "I believe we should, but I'll defer to your judgement, Professor."

"Sounds like a plan, Major," Smith said. "I don't want the helicopter crew left defenseless."

"The thing only seems to react when we get close to the building, or it," said Major Jones. "But I have no desire to test that theory. I'll detail Alderson and Beckett to take charge of the camp while the rest of us move out. Leftenant, Sergeant-Major, take charge and set up your best defenses here. Men! Form up and prepare to move out! Devon, Pitts, see to your men. Leave a squad here to protect the camp."

Moments later, we were on the move.

We marched in silence. In a tight group, we made our way up the trail to the pyramid. Once we got there, Sergeants Devon and Pitts busied themselves with instructing us in setting up our little trap. We lined up the grenades in shallow holes, then strung the tripwires to pull their pins far enough away from them so that the beast would have time to be almost on top of them when they detonated. Sergeant-Major Heath, Major Jones, and the Professor went right up to the pyramid's doors and started setting up their little surprise package. From where I was working on tripwires, it looked like they had cobbled together several packets of C4 and four canteens that had been filled with some kind of gooey tar kind of stuff. They used branches from the surrounding brush to hang the canteens on, not too near the plastique. They unscrewed the tops of the canteens and put detonators inside them, then resealed the caps. They tied everything together with what I overheard Heath say was "det cord." My best guess was that the canteens held a home-made version of napalm that the explosives were supposed to scatter along the building's walls. Heath had a little bucket of the stuff, and was using clumps of grass he pulled up to paint the doors with its contents. Too bad we couldn't open the thing's doors. Well, they kinda looked like doors, anyway.

I'm betting the insides of the building could be improved if we could have decorated it with some napalm. That'd get the beast's attention, anyway. Heath, Jones, and the Professor ran some wires off to the edge of the clearing to a spot behind a clump of rocks just big enough for one man to hide behind. Looking at it, I figured that there was going to be an argument as to who was going to be stationed there with the detonator plunger. Sure enough, they wanted the old man to set off the explosives. He objected, wanting to be in the thick of things. Somehow, the Major convinced him he was the best man for the job. From the look on Smith's face, he was none too happy with Major Jones' attempt at protecting him.

We finished with the grenades and tripwires, piled a huge bunch of underbrush against the sides and back of the pyramid's walls, and as per Major Jones' orders, deployed around the clearing to whatever cover we could find. We faced outward; watching for the beast. The Major lit a flare scavenged from the helicopter crew, and dashed around the pyramid lighting the underbrush, then turned and lofted the flare to the flat top of the pyramid. The flare didn't seem to trigger the trap that cost us Private Parker. The smoke from the burning underbrush boiled up and outward. Hopefully, the monster would see it and come running.

We heard a roar. The damn thing had seen the smoke.

"Look alive, Lads!" Major Jones shouted.

I heard a crashing through the underbrush outside the clearing. The thing seemed to be circling around to come up the trail from our camp. Good, it'd hit our tripwires then. Another roar, and the beast burst into sight from down the trail. It ran straight for the pyramid. Toward the only side we hadn't set fire to. It staggered as it hit the first tripwire, then recovered and kept going.

Our grenades went off like a string of firecrackers. I think we hurt it. It roared again as it got closer to the building. The professor waited until the last minute, then set off the C4. The explosion knocked the beast on its ass as the improvised napalm caught fire and exploded in turn. The thing was splattered with burning chemicals. It *whined* in pain as it regained its feet.

We ran around the building until we could all see the thing, then opened up on it with everything we had. Everyone unloaded on it at the same time. We only stopped firing when we had to reload. Fur and flesh and blood and gore flew away from the beast. It was like shooting fish in a barrel. I saw one of its arms fly off, then a leg, then someone got one of the explosive rounds dead-center into its open mouth. Its head dissolved into a cloud of bloody gobbets. We kept on firing at it until every round we had was expended. When the smoke and haze cleared, the thing was a pile of burning fur and flesh.

"Clear!" Major Jones shouted. We waited, ceasing fire as ordered. The Professor walked up to the thing, pulled a huge Bowie knife from his belt, and stabbed the remains of the beast square into what was left of its chest. Working the knife like a sword, he cut deep into the thing, then reached in with his other hand and pulled a silver, softball-sized sphere from its chest.

The building groaned.

"Fall back!" Major Jones shouted. We turned and ran for our lives. The pyramid lit up like a Christmas tree, shrieked and groaned as if it were in deathly pain, then slowly dissolved into nothing before our very eyes. The still burning brush along its sides and the flare from its rooftop collapsed inward as if the building had never been there at all. Finally, the fires died.

"I do believe we've won," Sergeant-Major Heath said. "Now, to count the cost…"

Professor Smith and Major Jones went into a huddle, talking quietly, but what seemed to me to be fiercely. Heath, Pitts, and Devon kept us from getting close to them. Finally, the Professor surrendered the sphere he'd pulled from the beast's chest to Major Jones. Jones wrapped the ball in tinfoil, then put it into the scorched, burned-out pail the napalm had been in, covering the pail with more tinfoil.

"Let's get the bloody hell out of here," said the Major.

We walked, and limped, back to camp. The next day, we broke camp and flew back to Base. Evidently, paperwork was filed and the surviving US soldiers from our little camping trip were inducted into the Major's little unit. Advanced a grade in rank, too.

I caught the old man loading up his truck to leave the day after we returned to base.

"What did we do? What did we win? What *was* that thing?" I asked him.

"If you know what's good for you," he replied as he got into his truck. "You'll forget this entire incident—or at least never mention it to anyone, ever. And just to make sure you don't have any 'difficulties' in the future, forget you ever met me. As far as you're concerned, this whole thing never happened. The pyramid never existed, the monster never existed, you were on a routine training mission with the Major's unit. No one died, no one saw anything, and no one *knows* anything. *Capiche?* You'll be watched for a long time. Best to never draw attention to yourself."

"Burn before reading?" I asked.

"Yeah," he replied. "Burn before reading. You know the drill. This'll be so far above Top Secret that it'd be more than your life is worth to even admit it happened. You've got the rest of your life ahead of you. Don't fuck it up."

"Will I ever see you again?" I asked.

"Probably not," Smith said. "No one will admit that *I* exist, either, so don't ask questions. You've got your whole life ahead of you. Just live it. Live it to the best of your ability. Then, who knows? Nothing is written in stone. Oh, about that Cuban scientist?"

"Yeah?" I replied.

"Let somebody else rescue him and his daughter. Don't go near it. That one is gonna be a disaster. You don't need that. Just walk away. And son?"

"Yeah?" I said again.

"Been a pleasure serving with you. Now go get something to eat. You're too skinny. They never feed you in the Army?"

Professor Smith started his truck and sped away. I had a feeling I'd see him again one day. Or maybe it was more than a feeling—a hope, maybe. I headed off towards the chow hall…

Closing Time

"I was getting tired of it all. Maybe it was time to retire.
If they'd let me get out in anything short of a body bag
and an unmarked grave…"
— Tom Darby.

I was beginning to feel my age. Wasn't so much the number of the years, as it was the wear and tear. I was slowing down. My reflexes weren't as sharp as they used to be.

I heard tires screeching behind me, car doors opening, and running footsteps. I spun around. My Colt was in my hand before I even had time to think of drawing it. Four men in dark suits, coming at me fast. Two held guns, one held a black bag—like a hood—and the last held what looked like a cattle prod. My Colt barked, then barked again. The two with guns went down. A third shot took Bag-Boy just above his knee. The guy with the cattle prod tripped, stumbled, and gave me time to aim more carefully. His right shoulder would never work again.

I backed to the wall behind me as I scanned the rest of the street—just in case they had any backup. Nothing in sight. I put a fresh magazine in the Colt and pocketed the partial. I wanted to look at their car, but my training took over, so I popped the lock on the nearest shop door and ducked inside. Good thing the shop was closed. I saw it was a candy store and hoped there wasn't anyone in the back. I went straight back through 'til I got to the shipping door in the back wall. It opened onto an alley wide enough for a delivery truck—but just barely. I went down the alley towards the direction I'd come. Checked the street it led to, holstered the Colt, and wound a tricky path back to my hotel. You better believe I checked reflections in shop windows every step of the way. If someone was tailing me, they were good. Once I got into my room, I reloaded the partial magazine from earlier, grabbed my bag, and snuck out of the hotel. I had paid for a week, up front, so the manager was going to get two days' worth of me not being there.

What the Hell just happened? I'm not even on an assignment, I thought.

Once I was safely inside the third-choice back-up safe house, I set up some simple boobytraps on the door to my room, then took a quick shower. As I let my hair dry, I checked over my remaining inventory of gear. A couple of packs of plastique, five detonator charges for same, 389 rounds of ammo—seven boxes in my pack and three magazines' worth—in my jacket pockets and chambered, my Colt, two knives, that fancy straight razor I picked up in Jamaica, bits of wire and a ball of twine, my clothes, a little gym bag, three different IDs, and somebody had put a bullet through my favorite fedora. *Damn it! I liked that hat!*

The phone rang.

"Empty Arms Hotel," I answered on the fifth ring.

"You're lucky to be alive," someone who sounded vaguely Eastern European said over the phone. *Not Russian, more like Polish or Romanian,* I thought as I listened to their accent. "You have a way of upsetting some very powerful people. One of them has decided you are too great a threat. I disagree. Meet me at the café where you normally have lunch. I will explain then." They hung up. *Great,* I thought, *Belgium was supposed to be boring…*

"Damn," I said aloud. "Been in this business too long. Everything looks like a trap." *He never said where to meet. 'The place where I normally have lunch…' I always vary my routine to keep from having a habitual place to be tracked to. I've never had lunch at the same place twice… Here, anyway… So, what have we got? Well for one thing, I need to get the hell out of Belgium, pretty damn quickly. Somehow, I've been tracked. This was supposed to be a vacation. I'm not on a mission—I'm on leave. Wait—where do I have lunch the most often? In the whole damned world? 'Normally,' he said. 'Normally,' for me, means some base or some facility back home.* "This is a pretty puzzle," I said to myself. "Time to get a move on, though. Escape and evade—that's the ticket."

I packed up my stuff and headed for the service elevator. Halfway there, I decided to use the stairs and go down two floors. *Then* I used the service elevator, but only as far as the second floor. Making my way to the back of the building, I used the fire escape to reach the hotel's loading dock for their deliveries. I hope the hotel doesn't mind the window latch I left unlocked on their fire escape. Once I was free of any prying eyes on the loading dock, I took a random path through a dozen back alleys. Mixing with the locals, once I made my way to a main street, as few locals as there were this time of day, I finally took a taxi out to the airport, booked a flight to London, and from there, eventually, back to the US. Took me three days, and I spent a sleepless night at Gatwick airport to make my eight AM redeye flight back to the US. I wound up in Atlanta, waiting on a connecting flight to Dallas. On a whim, I rented a car instead. Wasn't my money, anyway. This trip had burned up four perfectly good fake identities, one of which I bought from a dealer who ostensibly ran an ice cream shop in Gatwick airport. It pays to have connections, sometimes. I drove north from Atlanta to Chattanooga, then east to Knoxville. Spent the night in a fleabag motel in LaFollette. I remembered the town from one of my previous mission briefings. Nice to see what it actually looked like. The next day I was off north again to Kentucky. From there I headed to Langley, Virginia. Pulled off the road short of CIA headquarters and made a few discrete phone calls. One of them gifted me with a password to use at the guard shack at CIA Langley. Once inside the building, I met up with my old friend Joe.

We met in some dinky conference room instead of an office. I gathered he was as much of a visitor there as I was. We had a couple of cups of coffee while making small talk about old times. Eventually, I put the question to him.

"What was that kidnap-squad in Belgium all about? And who was the voice on the phone that wanted to meet me?"

"Remember that bank robbery in Greece you accidentally attended?" Joe asked. "The one you foiled and almost blew your cover for the real reason you were in Greece?"

"That one took some heavy bribes to cover up, yeah," I said. "Eventually everyone was 'convinced' that I was just a harmless US Army vet who happened to be in the wrong place at the wrong time. But what's the connection?"

"You beat the crap out of seven guys," Joe said. "In full view of a lobby full of bank employees and customers—"

"Three guys," I replied. "The other four shot each other while I was busy."

"That was a MAFIA job," said Joe. "Some big-wheel got pissed off that you busted up his little party. Now, remember the Italian girl you spent the weekend with right after that? *She* was his favorite mistress. He put a contract out on you. One of his lieutenants was on vacation and recognized you in Belgium. He called in some of his playmates. As for the guy on the phone, we're still trying to get a line on him. That was more than a little weird, to tell the truth. Even from everything you gave us in your report, we can't tie him, whoever he was, to anything else—at all. Best guess, he's Russian MAFIA, in competition with the Sicilian mob, and was going to bag you as a peace offering to the Sicilians. Worst case scenario, he's KGB and somebody like me, pulling who knows how many strings behind several sets of curtains— at least one of them Iron, if you get my drift."

"I'm getting too old for this shit," I said.

"I'm thinking along similar lines," Joe said. "Maybe you should retire. At least temporarily."

"Have we got a retirement plan that *doesn't* involve a body bag?" I asked.

"I said temporary, didn't I? You're too sharp an op to lose forever."

"Thanks—I think," I said. "What do you have in mind?"

'Nothing drastic," Joe said. "And nothing irreversible. Just someplace out of the way doing something quiet—at least for a while."

"I'm all ears," I replied.

"We've got a little branch office down in Georgia," Joe said. "Quiet, peaceful, and practically invisible. I can get you a spot down there to lay low for a few years."

"What are you doing with an office in Georgia?" I asked.

"It's not just us," Joe said. "All the 'alphabet' agencies got together and worked up a plan to make something like a safe house--but spread out all over the country. You're not the first person to get too hot to keep active, but too valuable to 'misplace.' Little towns all over the place have something like this going on. If a place is quiet enough, sleepy enough, but still big enough so that strangers can come and go unnoticed, then they were considered for this kind of branch office."

"Sounds weird—like that 60s TV show with the actor from Secret Agent Man," I said.

"Sort of like that, yeah, but nobody's a prisoner," Joe said. "It's more like a loose, unsupervised network that happens to be in one general area. Sorta like being in deep cover, but not behind any enemy lines, you're here at home. Out of sight and out of mind, so to speak. But you'll have to create your own cover ID and get a job to make it look normal. That way there aren't any records up here that can be compromised. And we can leak a fake KIA or MIA report that anyone looking for the *real* you should buy into."

"Should?" I asked.

"Nothing is foolproof," Joe said. "The branch office's cover is a small garage, outside of Athens. Close enough so you can get to it to check in every so often—without attracting attention. I'd suggest you get a place outside of town, but close enough so you can go enjoy the nightlife, maybe catch a few football games. Far enough outside of town so maybe you can do some fishing and hunting—like you used to do back home when you were a kid. The pay from us is enough to get by on, but you can supplement that with whatever you can find down there that takes your fancy. You'd just be a regular working stiff, doing whatever you like to pass the time. You don't have to work at the garage. Just check in there from time to time. Get your car's oil changed—whatever."

"So, I go down there, get a job for butter and egg money, rent an apartment or whatever, and lay low for a while?" I asked. "And I get a little retirement money too, in whatever bank account I set up?"

"Your GI pension, medical insurance, *and* a stipend from us, but set up for whatever cover you create. I'll see to the paperwork personally. Up here, you'll just be a number, just another account on the books. Nothing to tie you to any work you've done for us since Korea. Your new identity will go in the computers as another Korean War veteran, same rank, paygrade, and benefits, but a different name."

"I'm tempted," I said. "I won't miss the excitement. This job is a tad rough on your nerves."

"You're only in your 40s," Joe said. "Still in good health and deserving a normal life. I can make sure you don't get called back up unless there's a huge emergency—end of the world stuff. Barring something unforeseeable, you could even ride it out for the rest of your life."

"I won't miss someone trying to kill me twice a month, that's for sure," I said.

"We got a deal?" Joe asked.

"Sounds like a plan," I said. "Where do I sign?"

The biggest change I had to make to Joe's retirement plan was not making up a new name. Thanks to the records department Joe had an in with, there were now *two* grunts named Tom Darby in Korea at the same time. My old life went into the new identity instead of me having to get used to a new name. I was still a former fighter pilot, but there weren't any records of *me* getting press-ganged into working with the Spooks. That was the *other* guy. Since I'd done most of my work on the ground under cover identities, Joe thought it would work—although he was hard to convince for a while. Eventually, he saw some possibilities in giving my official records to a fictitious distant cousin. It was all just enough to throw off any possible search for me—the *real* me, I mean. *My* records now say that I retired from the Air Force after Korea, went into the construction industry, and drifted around the country as a carpenter and house painter. Good, honest work that I actually have some skill doing. Growing up on a farm *is* kind of like advanced vocational training in a lot of practical jobs, anyway.

Once all the paperwork was underway, I shook Joe's hand and set off to house-hunt in the counties bordering on Athens. I finally settled on a rental off of the Jefferson Road north of Athens. I was about 15 minutes outside of town. The place wasn't much to look at, but it had a little kitchen, a big living room, a fair-sized bedroom, and a tiny bathroom & a big closet. I went into Athens several times and prowled the charity stores for used furniture. At the same time, I got myself a job as a house painter with one of the local construction companies. I kept my motorcycle at the house under a tarp, bought an old beater pickup truck from an old farmer nearby. Paying cash for that stuff helped keep me off the radar, but I did have to surface to get tags and insurance. In just a few weeks, I had the house furnished and established myself as a painter. I also did some carpentry to fill in the lean times between painting jobs. I got a lot of work in town helping fix up some old houses that college students were renting while they went to school at the local University. I got invited to a lot of college parties that way. Someone would plan a kegger, hire a local band, and throw a party to celebrate getting their house renovated, the football team winning a game, or even any random day ending in Y, so to speak.

It didn't take long before I'd befriended several of the local musicians working those parties, I got a reputation as someone willing to pitch in and help tote amplifiers out of whoever's van or truck—helping the bands set up for gigs. Eventually, I found myself doing the same thing at local bars and clubs. I did construction during the day whenever that was available, went home and cleaned up, then back to town to be a roadie at night. I got to hear a lot of the bands that eventually got big.

That's how I got to meet Alice. She was an Art teacher at the University. She liked the party scene, the bands, the students, but being a teacher meant that she really couldn't have much of a romantic life. Not unless she wanted to date another professor, or something like that. Long black hair, blue eyes, tall and a little on the skinny side, but still prettier than she thought she was. I'd seen her around at several of the clubs, a few of the parties, and a couple of times at thrift stores when I was looking for knick-knacks to clutter up the shelves in my little house. Eventually, we got to talking. I found out that she liked the same kind of books as I did, went to the same movies as I did, and was working on a book she hoped would make her name in Art History circles. The first time we got to talk, she was fending off the advances of a drunken frat boy who basically just wanted to carve another notch on his bedpost, so to speak. I stepped up and offered to buy her a drink just as Frat Boy's current girlfriend barged up and started a shouting match with him at the bar. I knew the bartender, gave him a knowing look and a sideways nod of my head indicating Frat Boy, then watched as the bartender signaled the bar's bouncers to amble up and ask Frat Boy and Miss Girlfriend to leave before the cops had to take notice of them.

"Sorry about that," I said to her. "Buy you a drink?"

She looked me over, evidently decided she liked what she saw, and told Tony—the bartender—to give her a Boilermaker.

"On me, Tony, and make that two if you'd be so kind," I said.

"You're with the band, aren't you?" Tony asked me.

"I just help unload the van and set up the amps," I replied. "Nothing special. Just a little side money. They're good kids. I think they're gonna go far, one day."

Tony nodded and set two mugs of beer and two shot glasses of tequila in front of Alice and I. I passed him a ten and told him to give us a refill in a little while.

"What's your game?" Alice asked after telling me her name and asking for mine.

"I'm just a working stiff," I said. "I sling a hammer and a paintbrush for a living. Work for Ballenger's Construction, most of the time. Pays the bills and keeps food on the table."

"I teach Art History," she said. "A few lectures a week, some slide shows for the students to get to know what styles are what, and grading exams. Dull as ditchwater, mostly. I've seen you around somewhere. The antique store?"

"Potter's House," I said. "I pick up a few brass bits of junk, maybe find some Chinese lacquer-work that's pretty. Just dust-catchers to dress up my home a little bit, really. I remember seeing you there, from time to time."

"I'm flattered you noticed me," she said.

"You're difficult to overlook," I said. "Kinda stand out in a crowd, if you don't mind my saying."

"Oh, you're a silver-tongued devil, aren't you?"

"First I've heard that," I said, smiling. We drained our drinks and I caught Tony's eye for a refill. Once we had fresh drinks, we headed for one of the few empty tables. Just happened to be near the door so we could hear each other talk above the band. We lingered over our Boilermakers, talked a lot, got refills when necessary, and passed the night talking until the bar shut down.

"I gotta go help the band pack up," I said. "Maybe we can do this again sometime?"

"I think I'd like that," she replied. She fumbled in her purse for a pen and then wrote down her phone number. "I'm busy the rest of the week, but call me Friday night?" She passed the note to me and I carefully put it away.

"Count on it," I said. "I'll most likely be road crew for another band, but if you don't mind meeting at whatever club they're playing we can pick up where we left off."

"It's a date," she said. She blushed a little, but smiled. Then she got up and walked away. I watched her sashay to the door, admiring the way her hips swayed as she walked. I got up to go help the band load their van.

This could be the start of something big, I thought as I walked towards the stage. Once the band drove off, I walked to my truck and headed back to my little house. For the first time, home seemed empty, but my thoughts were warm and full.

I called Alice on Friday afternoon about 5:30, just like I promised. I had to use the pay phone at the gas station about two miles from my house 'because I still hadn't gotten a phone installed at the rental. I figured if the landlady wanted a phone there, she'd foot the bill herself. For what I was paying for the place every month, she could well afford it. I wasn't going to spring for all the upfront costs of having a phone installed for a place I was just renting. Not my circus, not my monkeys.

Alice and I made arrangements to meet up at the club the band I was working for were playing that night. She knew I'd be there *way* before the show started so I could help the band set up for their gig. She showed up about when the band was ready to play their first set. Call it 7:30 or so. We had a few drinks, danced a bit, then split up when it was time for me to help the band with the load-out. We made another date for the next week before we went our separate ways. I got back to my empty, lonely house about 2 AM. I laid out my work clothes for the next day, climbed into my little thrift-store bed, and dreamed of Alice until my alarm clock jingled its bells to get me up for my regular workday.

Work was dull, as usual, but I did my normal best efforts. We finished up the last house in the development that day. At the end of the day, my boss was hesitant to tell the crew where to meet up for the next day's job, but finally admitted that the market was slowing down and he didn't exactly have a new job site for us to go to. He promised us that the market would pick back up soon, though. I wasn't too worried, since I was only working to keep my cover alive. After all, I still had my retirement money coming in from my old life. I could have just lived off of that and no one would be the wiser, but having a cover is always good.

I'd gotten a pager to let me know when the boss wanted to get in touch with me. If it went off, I'd have to drive to the gas station to call back, but that was just how things worked at the time. I made a mental note to start house-hunting for a place closer to town that would have a phone.

The construction crew didn't work again until a few days later when the boss had snagged a contract to remodel one of the big old houses on a back street near Fraternity Row on Milledge Avenue. It was a big old place. We had to redo a lot of wiring to get it up to code, and we spent weeks tearing out walls to replace when the electricians were finished. I got a lot of work hours repainting the refinished walls.

Meanwhile, Alice and I were stepping out together every Friday. Some weeks I got to take her to dinner during the middle of the week at one of the restaurants instead of just meeting up on weekends at a club where I was helping a band. We got to know each other really well. Eventually, one weekend she stayed at the club until I was through loading up the band's gear. As the band drove off, she looked me in the eye and asked "your car or mine?"

Suddenly, I was introduced to something I'd missed out on by going into the Army before I was old enough to finish High School; necking in a car. Old as I was, making out in a car was a new experience for me. Her VW bug wasn't a whole lot larger than the cockpit of my Saber jet, but it proved to be a *lot* more fun. Neither one of us thought a "no-tell motel" was a good idea.

Eventually, she invited me back to her house in Colbert instead of us making do in a parking lot in Athens. It was a big old house in a quiet neighborhood on what she called the "poor side" of the railroad tracks. Poor being a relative term is what I thought once I'd seen the place. It was located in behind the Post Office, on a side road that eventually went out to a covered bridge that hadn't long been a State Park. Her house was a two story, twelve room mansion built either before the Civil War, or a reproduction built during the 1920s when that style was in vogue again.

Looking at the place in the late-night Autumn moonlight, I could well believe that it was a century old, or more.

"This is yours?" I asked.

"I rent it," she replied with a giggle. "The owner is a little old lady who lives in a retirement community in Florida. I rent it from her granddaughters. They live in a mansion back in the ritzy part of Athens, over behind Five Points. They call this their Summer Cottage." Alice laughed again, then led me inside. Once over the threshold, she locked the door, hung up her coat, took mine and hung it up too, then we were in each other's arms.

Seems like only a minute later, we were peeling each other's clothes off, right there in the foyer. Somehow, we managed to make it up the staircase to her bedroom. The rest of the night was a bit of a blur, but a really pleasant one. I know we made love over and over again until the sun started peeking through the windows. After that, we slept in each other's arms until late afternoon.

That whole weekend was like a dream come true. I know we cooked for each other in the house's surprisingly modern kitchen, showered, lay together while we caught our breath, and somehow totally avoided wearing any clothes until her alarm clock woke us on Monday morning in time for her to get ready to go teach her classes at the University. She took it as given that I was going to move into her house, so I spent my free time during the next week bringing my few belongings over to her place. I told my landlady that I was moving out of my little rental, paid her a month's rent that I wasn't going to be there to use, and turned in my keys once the house was empty.

Alice had a phone, so I was able to tell my boss to call there instead of using my pager. I also told my contacts in the various bands I worked with how to get in touch with me when they needed me. Then I went out to a pay phone and called Joe's garage to update them as to my changing situation.

"Hello?" I said. "This is Tom. May I speak with Clayton?"

"Sure thing," said the voice on the other end of the phone. "Wait one, he's washing his hands after finishing up an oil change on a Fiat…"

"Clayton here," came a reply after just a few minutes' wait time. "Tommy-Boy, what can we do for you?"

"I think I need my brakes checked, they're starting to squeak," I replied. That was a code phrase to tell Clay that I needed to file a change of status report.

"On the truck or on the bike?" Clay asked. Another code phrase that was asking if this concerned my new identity or my original one.

"On my truck," I said, indicating my new identity.

"We've got an opening on Thursday," Clay said. "But if you can come in before lunchtime today maybe Bobby can take a look at it." Meaning that I should come to the garage right now and file the paperwork.

"I'll be there inside of an hour," I said, meaning that I'd be there as quickly as I could drive there.

"OK, I'll tell Bobby to take lunch early. See you then," Clay said, then hung up the phone. Which meant that I'd better get a move on. Thankfully, I had learned a lot of the local back roads and could get to the garage in less than half an hour—if I didn't mind driving like a bat out of hell along three or four deserted back roads. I hung up the phone, got in my truck, and lit out hell for leather.

I made it to the garage on the Commerce Road in record time. Once I parked, I made my way to the office. Clay was expecting me, so we didn't linger too long before the soundproof door of his little office was closed and locked.

"What's up?' Clay asked. I told him about Alice and how things had gotten serious between us. I also gave him the address and phone number of Alice's house in Colbert.

"I'll have to run a check on her, but that's just SOP. You getting serious about this girl? Sounds healthy and normal, and like more fun than a barrel of monkeys." Clay laughed. Then he got serious. "Look, chances are she's exactly who and what you think she is. We're a *long* way from the front lines of the Cold War nowadays. Got to run the check, regardless, but I doubt we'll find anything. So relax, let things happen, and just enjoy yourselves. It's about time you found out what you've been fighting for all these years is all about. Now, what about work?"

"The housing market is on the decline," I said. "I can get jobs with restoration crews since I have a reputation as a craftsman, but I don't dare flash as much cash as I really have or I'll attract attention. I'll have to live poor for a while. At least act like I'm living off of my pension as a Korean vet. No flashy sports cars, no yachts, no vacations to anywhere outside the country. I know the drill."

"And no going anyplace *inside* the country you've ever been to for an assignment, either," said Clay.

"Damn," I said. "Daytona is out, then." I laughed. "Maybe a week in some RV park in the Smoky Mountains will float her boat instead."

"Good luck," Clay said. "Women that will accept a vacation in the mountains instead of at the beach are few and far between these days."

"Understood," I said, grinning. "We've about covered everything I can think of. You got anything?"

"Not unless you can get me tickets to that Mother's Finest concert next month that the radio's been squawking about all damn day. My wife loves them," Clay replied.

"That's the big leagues," I said. "I work with the small fry. REM, the B-52s, Love Tractor, Pylon… I can get you into one of their shows."

"Who knows?" Clay said. "Maybe one of these days one of them will make the big time."

"Only time will tell," I said as I stood up to leave. "Miracles do happen, after all."

I decided to go get some lunch downtown, since I was so close already. I aimed the truck Southward on 441, and made good time until I got to the overpass where 441 went under the Athens Bypass. I took a few of the back roads through neighborhoods that looked like they hadn't changed much since the roaring '20s. Every few blocks I went past an antebellum mansion or two. Athens is like that; some of the houses have been standing since the 1800s. After a couple of twists and turns, I came out on Prince Avenue near a big granite church. I turned left and went a couple of blocks until I could see the left turn onto Milledge Avenue. *Almost there,* I thought. I pulled into the little parking lot for the Taco Stand, found a spot that I could back the truck out of pretty easily, and went inside. I chowed down on a big taco, a combo burrito, and finished up with a spinach quesadilla. I took my time over lunch. I knew Alice wouldn't be home until late afternoon. Her last class wouldn't start until four in the afternoon, wouldn't end until 5:30, and thanks to rush-hour traffic out of town she wouldn't make it home before quarter after six. After lunch, I stopped at the Bi-Lo grocery on North Avenue to pick up something to cook for her for supper. I figured I could have something ready for her about the same time she pulled into her driveway—as long as what I bought wasn't too fancy to cook. I walked out with pork chops, a can of sauerkraut, a can of applesauce, and some dinner rolls. Nothing too challenging, if I could remember how momma made it. The drive from the store to Alice's house went pretty quickly for me since it was just before the 3:00 afternoon rush hour of people leaving the local factories to head home. Once I got to the house, I rambled around in Alice's kitchen and found she had a pressure cooker. I layered the pork chops and sauerkraut in the cooker, put in just enough water to keep things from scorching, and got it on the stove. I figured I could start the oven pre-heating by the time she was starting for home. That way the rolls would be ready as soon as she walked in the door.

I timed everything just about perfectly. I was draining the water out of the pressure cooker when she pulled into the driveway. By the time she changed out of her work clothes and came back downstairs, I was putting stuff on plates. She had a couple of bottles of that white wine she likes that she'd bought on her way home. Turned out it went great with the chops and kraut.

"You're more domesticated than I thought," she said while we were eating. "A girl could get used to this."

"Momma insisted that all of us learned to cook—at least a little bit," I answered. "I can't do much of anything fancy, but I don't have to depend on any restaurants to survive. Daddy said he'd stick to the BBQ grill, but he got pretty good at making breakfast in the kitchen on Sunday mornings while Momma got ready for church. But then, eggs and bacon and whatnot aren't all that hard. I never mastered biscuits, but my cornbread is fairly good." Just then, the phone rang. Alice got up to answer it, then called me to come to the phone. It was a guy with one of the bands I worked with. Turns out I could help with the set-up and load-out at a club in Athens on Friday night. Wouldn't pay much, but every little bit helps. I hated pretending I was almost broke all the time. Cover IDs work that way, sometimes. I couldn't let on that I was pretty well off with the retirement pay and the bonuses coming in. Couldn't afford to attract attention, flashing cash around, so these under-the-table jobs for spare cash came in handy. I told Alice about the gig while we finished supper. She was interested in coming to the club to see the band.

"I'll have to be there about the time you get off from work," I told her. "If you want to come home and change clothes, the club will probably be opening the doors by the time you could drive back into town."

"Probably be best if I just went straight to the club from work," she said. "No use wasting gas. I can redo my make-up once my last class ends. Nobody will think anything about it. Some of the other girls at work use the restrooms there to get ready for a night out with their boyfriends. I won't be able to take a shower, but teaching isn't sweaty work, anyway."

"You won't be bored?" I asked. "The band won't start playing until after dark. I mean, once I'm finished helping them set up, I'll be able to sit with you. I think the club has sandwiches and whatnot, though. I've had a pretty good roast beef sandwich there, with chips and a pickle slice, but it's not gonna be like a restaurant."

"Which club?" Alice asked.

"Tyrone's," I replied. "Used to be the Chameleon, I've been told."

"I know the place," Alice said. "It was the Potter's House thrift store—about five years ago. I used to walk to the Chameleon for a ham omelet for lunch, some days. It's less than a mile from the Art School. Have to park somewhere along one of the back streets near it, though. I don't fancy walking back to the University to get my car after closing time."

"I never knew that," I said. "But then, I'm pretty new in town. Want another glass of wine?"

"Maybe after we do the dishes," she said. "I want to open the other bottle when we've got time to relax."

"I'll wash, you dry?" I said.

"Deal," Alice said. She giggled as she got up and helped me take our plates to the sink.

"What's so funny?" I asked as I ran the water to get it hot.

"Us," she said. "Me. I've never felt so comfortable being with someone before." She passed me the stopper for the sink, then the dish detergent.

"Well," I replied. "I've never felt this comfortable being with somebody, either. Maybe that's a good sign?"

"Let's just take things as they come," Alice said. "I've had too many relationships blow up in my face before. Makes me kinda nervous that everything's going so well."

Blow up in your face? I thought. *Lady, you have NO idea how many things have blown up in MY face...*

Once we had the dishes in the drainer to finish drying, she turned to me, looked me in the eyes, then asked "Are you ready for dessert?"

"I didn't think about dessert," I said. "I should have made something."

"I've been thinking about it *all* day," she replied. "I know *exactly* what I want, too." She took my hand, led me out of the kitchen, and up the stairs to her—*our* bedroom, the second bottle of wine and two glasses in her other hand...

The rest of the night passed *very* pleasantly.

I got a call the next morning after Alice left for work. It was one of the contractors I knew. He wanted me to come and do a little painting at one of the big old houses on Fraternity Row, on Milledge Avenue. I put on my work clothes and headed towards town.

The job was a minor kitchen remodel. All the plumbing work had been done, a new sink and countertop installed, and all I needed to do was paint three walls of the kitchen to match the new color scheme. The Frat boys were all out of the way, in classes, so I made quick work of it. I was finished before the afternoon was too far gone. I took the wad of twenties my boss-*du jour* handed me when I was done, then headed out to a little place nearby uptown where I could get a drink and some food. Two chili dogs and a beer later, I was bored and headed for one of the bars uptown. Once I got there, I found trouble. Nothing big, just some guy trying to pick up a girl. Trouble was, she was already spoken for. He was being as persuasive as he could, but she wasn't buying it. *Then,* her boyfriend came in. Dude looked like a linebacker for the college football team. Big, broad-shouldered, muscled up, and more than a little peeved that some flashy-dressed dufus was hitting on his girl. I thought there was gonna be a fight, but the dufus backed down and retreated to a table next to mine. He was muttering under his breath in some Arabic dialect. Thing is, he had a British accent to his English. I figured him for a rich spoiled brat who was here on a foreign exchange student gig. I understood enough of his Arabic to get the picture. He was not used to being told "no." Especially by a little slip of a girl who just happened to have a protector who looked like he could tear in half anyone who pissed him off. I made the mistake of chuckling at his misfortune. He overheard me and angrily turned to face me.

"Is something funny?" he asked. "Do I amuse you?"

"Relax kid," I replied, putting my empty glass down carefully. "You just had the bad luck to come on to the girlfriend of one of the football players, that's all. Could happen to anybody. It's not like she's wearing a sign saying she's taken, after all. Honest mistake. Laugh it off. Big Boy over there could hand you your head without breaking a sweat, *and* not get in trouble with the police. He's a Golden Child in this town. The football team can get away with damn near anything. Lighten up and mark it down to a learning experience."

"Do you know who I am?" he asked.

"No," I replied. "But let me guess. You're someone rich and powerful—back wherever it is you come from. You're here as a foreign exchange student at the university, I'd guess. And you're used to getting your own way. No one ever tells you no, back home. And you don't like it when people here treat you like just another average Joe. Am I close?"

"I am Hassad al Amin—*Prince* Hassad al Amin, of Kuwait. True, I am a very minor Prince—a mere distant cousin of the present ruling family. I am *several* comfortable steps away from being in line for the throne—"

"But still, someone important, back home?" I asked, interrupting him before he could get into full flow.

"Indeed," he replied. "You are perceptive, for an American."

"I'll take that as a compliment," I said. "Whether it was intended or not. Prince Hassad, I am Tom Darby, late of the US Air Force, retired after the Korean War. I am *not* anyone of importance. Merely a retired pilot. Just another average Joe, not to put too fine a point on it. Your English tutor was British, I would guess from your accent."

"Yes, the British have always made great teachers—or so my father tells me."

"I would agree with your father on that account," I said. "I see that you are drinking beer. I am guessing that you are either a non-practicing Muslim, or a member of the Eastern Orthodox faith. May I buy you another round?"

"Eastern Orthodox, yes.," the prince replied. "And I would be most thankful for another drink."

"Please do me the honor of joining me at a table, then. I will go and fetch us a pitcher of beer, with which we may partake while we become better acquainted."

"You are a very strange man," said the prince. "I am beginning to like you."

"Miracles do happen," I said with a grin as I stood to go to the bar.

The prince and I spent the next two hours drinking and talking. Finally, I had to go home to Alice. It was her turn to cook, and I was looking forward to seeing what she had in mind—for supper, and afterward.

Supper was fried chicken, potato salad, pinto beans, and cornbread. There were tomato slices, Vidalia onion wedges, and a store-bought jar of chow-chow to accompany everything. Alice turned out to be a far better cook than I. As we ate, I told her about my day. She'd heard of the prince—he had a reputation among the Sorority Sisters on campus. They thought he was a bit of a creep, but money changes everything. She'd never met him herself, though. I warned her he was an arrogant, womanizing little prick.

"That's what the girls tell me too," she said. "A real Don Juan type. Love 'em and leave 'em. He's got a reputation on campus."

"Well, he's so self-centered he thinks the world revolves around him," I said. "But one day he's gonna try and seduce the wrong girl and get his ass beat by her boyfriend."

"I believe you're right," Alice said. "He's too pushy. One day he's going to get himself in trouble."

That turned out to be a prophecy, but Alice and I spent the night in far different pursuits. Art, for one, she was teaching me a bit about painting. Very gradually, but still—I'd bought a new leather bomber jacket and wanted some artwork on the back. I showed her an old photo I had of my father and I, out fishing on his boat, and she was teaching me how to use a grease pencil to draw on the leather so that I could eventually paint it up into something pretty nifty to show off to other bikers while I was off riding. Of course, once the lesson was done, we headed off up the stairs to pursue quite a different hobby...

Next morning, I woke up long enough to see Alice off to work, then I went back to bed. I had a long night in store for me tonight helping out the band. Just before noon, I got a call from another contractor friend. He'd not long ago bought a little apartment complex. It used to be a motel, way back when. All his tenants had finally vacated the place so he could refurbish it, at last. I gathered that he'd not been renting out the apartments as the tenants moved out. He had his own painting crew and carpenters, but they were all busy with other jobs. He offered me $200 to drop everything and come change all the locks on the apartment doors. I knew it was a thirty-room place, not counting the lobby, laundry room, and what used to be the office when it was a motel. There was also one of those lounge-type bars on the lowest floor of the place, but they were good clients and I didn't have to mess with their locks. I dickered him up to $300 to do 30 door locks and

60 deadbolts—and half the deadbolts were on sliding glass balcony doors, so they'd be smaller. He agreed, so long as I could do the job in one day. All I really needed for the job was a few screwdrivers, the new locks, and the old keys.

I was dressed and out the door in fifteen minutes. I stopped at a gas station on the way and got a pimento cheese sandwich and a cup of coffee. Within an hour I met my friend in the parking lot of his apartment building.

"Here's the keys," he said as I walked over and shook his hand. "I've got all the new locks here in my truck. Don't bother with the old office or the laundry room. I'm going to fix up the office for a friend of mine and let him live here as a security guard for the place. He's a Nam Vet, going through some tough times. He'll move in sometime next month—once I get the rooms fixed up for him. All I want is to get these locks changed—just in case someone didn't turn in all the keys they had for the old locks."

"No squatters needed," I said. "Good idea."

"Right," he answered. "Covering all the bases, so to speak. You think you can get it done today?"

"Won't take long," I said. "The balcony door locks will be the trickiest. I've got the tools to do the work, and a can of WD-40 in case something gets sticky. I should be done by 4:00 or so."

"Just leave the old locks and the keys inside the door of the office and lock up when you're done. I come back around 5 to pick 'em up. All the keys have the apartment numbers on them. Just swap the tags over to the new keys and everything will be hunky-dory. Here's your pay."

He handed over the money, then helped me move the boxes of locks over to my pick-up. I got started as he drove off. I got done with everything at about 3:30. Only one lock made me get out the WD. Only took me a few minutes each to do all the others. I locked everything up in my truck when I was done, then went around to the back of the place to get a beer at the bar.

The back parking lot sloped downward a bit. The motel had been built on a little hillside, with the bar taking the place of a basement for the motel rooms. It stuck out a bit from the rest of the building, so it has some nice window seating facing its parking lot. The other two floors of the place overhang the bar, with the office directly above it, and the rooms stretching off to the left of the office. There was a janitor's closet on each floor to make it an even 16 rooms on each floor.

The bar was pretty nice, for an older place. "The Lily Pad" was the name of the place. The bartender was friendly, the beer was cold, and I had the place pretty much to myself. It had a nice little baby grand piano off in one corner near the bar. The rest of the place was dotted with tables and chairs. As I was leaving, the piano player wandered in and started tinkling away on the piano. I could hear him as I walked around to the front of the building. I locked the old locks and the new keys up in the office, then drove home.

I took a quick shower, called the band's manager to see if the gig was still on for tonight, and worked on the painting on my leather jacket for a while. Once it was time to get ready, I got dressed to leave for the club. I met up with the band just before 6:00, and joined my roadie friends toting everything in and setting the band up for their gig. They did a sound check at about 7, and were ready for the gig in less than an hour. Alice came in while they were doing their sound check and we talked for a while at one of the little tables near the back where "friends of the band" hung out. We didn't drink much, so I was a little surprised that she got me to get up and dance a few times.

After midnight, the bar closed down and I helped with the load-out, then drove Alice back to her car. We got back to Colbert a little after 1 AM, had a drink, then went to bed. The phone woke us up at about 10. It was the garage, wanting me to come in "to check the truck's transmission." Code for a briefing they wanted me to have. Alice pouted dramatically for a few minutes, then laughed and perked up when I told her about a house party one of my painter friends had told me about that he highly recommended we go to that night. We parted ways pretty happily, and she promised me a plate of spaghetti when I got back.

I pulled into the garage parking lot about noon—or a bit later. Clay met me before I'd reached the door.

"Something's come up," he said. "Let's go to the office."

"What's up?" I asked when we got situated in Clay's office.

"I hear you've gotten friendly with some minor nobility," he began.

"Hassan?" I asked. "He's a jerk, but maybe being in the US will knock some of his rough edges off. What about him?"

"We're not allowed to get too close to him," Clay said. "But I'm glad you did. Even if it was by accident. He refused to bring any security with him from his home country. Plus, he refused to have any of our people hanging around him, too. He's out there all on his own. The Agency is concerned he might be too good a kidnap target for the other side to ignore."

"Possible, I suppose," I said. "But he's not a high-profile target, is he?"

"Not as such," said Clay. "But if you start hanging out with him, we could have a set of eyes and ears on the inside—just in case something *did* go tits-up"

"I'm supposed to be keeping a low profile, remember?" I asked. "I'm *officially* dead. If I get noticed, my cover is blown all to hell."

"Can't be helped," said Clay. "You lucked up into something we couldn't manage to pull off in a month of Sundays. We want you to keep an eye on the Prince, that's all."

"I can't drop everything and become his bodyguard, Clay. That's too public. Plus, this is supposed to be my retirement. If those mobsters catch on that I'm still alive—everyone I know becomes a target. You included! This whole operation of yours could become a target. I don't care if it's Sicilian or Russian Mafia—they don't play by anybody's rules but their own. And they play *rough!* Car bombs, assassins, drive-by shootings—all bets are off with those nuts."

"That's a given," Clay replied. "We're not asking you to move in with the guy. Just stay friendly with him. Hang out with him when you run into him. Keep an eye on him when you *do* run into him. Just play nice and see that nothing happens to him. His daddy wants him to have a babysitter. You're the closest thing we have to that. All I'm asking you to do is wing it for a while and keep him out of any um, difficulties."

I stood up and turned around, looking out Clay's office window into the interior of the garage. I took a deep breath and turned back around to face Clay.

"You're asking me to risk everything for the sake of a guy who really needs an ass-beating to adjust his attitude. Alice's life, *your* life, all your crew out there—for what? A few barrels of oil and a friend in the Middle East? Is it *that* important?"

"Yeah," said Clay. "I know what I'm asking."

"What you *need* to do is hook Hassan up with a girl," I said. "One of ours, an agent, one who is willing to sleep with him until he graduates and goes back home. All he *really* wants is to keep being a playboy until graduation. Might take a whole *string* of girls—but *that's* what you need."

"We don't *have* a girl," said Clay. "Not one we could ask to do *that,* anyway. Much less a whole string of 'em. All we have right now, is *you.* I can't *make* you do it. All I can ask you to do is become, and stay, the Prince's friend. For now, anyway. Just until we can get something better set up."

"That would be easy if he weren't an asshole," I said. "He's gonna get into a fight over some girl—you know that. It's only a matter of time."

"And that would cause an international incident," said Clay. "If it was hookers and blow, we could maybe contract something out. But Hassan likes *classy* girls—girl-next-door types. He doesn't want hookers—or there wouldn't be a problem. The New York office could hire a dozen girls to move down here and go to bed with him. But that's not what he *wants.* I *think* what he's really looking for is some sweet, ordinary but smart, 'typical' American girl he can take home to meet his family, marry him, and be queen of his little rat-hole country. Fits his profile, anyway."

"Oh—shit," I replied. "This is gonna get dirty. Mark my words, this *is* gonna blow up in our faces sooner or later."

"Just be his friend," Clay said. "Teach him how to find the girl of his dreams and quit chasing whichever skirt crosses his path."

"It'd be easier to teach him how to walk on water," I muttered under my breath.

"What?" asked Clay.

"Nothing," I answered. "Forget it. Just blowing off steam. Are we done here?"

"Yeah," said Clay. "You'll do it?"

"Did I ever have a choice?" I asked. "See you later…" I walked out and got in my truck. I cussed a blue streak all the way back to Colbert.

I put on a happy face for Alice as I went into the house. The spaghetti smelled wonderful, and tasted even better—she even had garlic bread and a bottle of Italian wine for us to have with it. I did my best to hide the ugly mood Clay had put me in. Maybe it worked—or maybe Alice just decided not to press me about what happened during my day. Just as we finished dinner, I got a call from the manager of one of the bands I roadie for, about a gig the next night. I'd be finished up with a painting job earlier the same afternoon, so I'd have time to come home and change before meeting up with the band. Alice wanted to meet up at the club the band was playing in, so we planned for that, too. The rest of the evening, we passed quite pleasantly. Alice showed me a few more art tricks for the painting on my jacket. After that, we played music and danced in the living room, holding each other close. Then as the night grew on towards midnight, we went upstairs to be a bit more romantic.

The next morning, I arrived early at the job site to get a start on the painting gig. The contractor met me in the parking lot of the building and let me in. All the furniture was already moved away from the walls and drop cloths covered both it and the floors. All I had to do was bring my gear in and start painting. Alice had made a lunch for me—sandwiches, chips and a thermos of coffee, so I didn't even have to leave the site for that. No one was around, no one to slow me down, and I made good time on the rooms I had to paint. By late afternoon, I was finished. I cleaned my brushes at the water spigot outside after I locked up the house, then headed for Colbert for a quick shower and change of clothes before heading back out to meet up with the band. We loaded up their van and the rental truck the manager had hired, and headed out to the club to start setting up. By the time they were doing their sound check, it had gotten dark outside. I had a couple of beers with the other folks on the road crew once we had the amps and instruments set up. I sometimes had a little bit of trouble finding things to talk about with the younger roadies—I avoided topics like the recently-ended war in Southeast Asia, for instance—because I was a generation older than most of them, but as long as we stuck to music and football and what else we did for a living everything was cool. The younger kids were still in High School when Nixon brought the troops home from Vietnam, I mean. They were taking classes at UGA, bitching about how much homework their professors assigned, praising the new bands starting to become known on the party circuit—stuff like that. One kid patiently explained to me the new "Punk Rock" stuff that was hitting the radio. The college radio station was one of the few I could reliably pick up on the radio in my old truck, so I'd heard some of it. I just tried to look interested and tried to fit in, you know?

Alice came in about half an hour before the show was due to start. I got us a table, then we ordered a plate from the bar's kitchen, and a pitcher of beer.

"This is a pretty good roast beef sandwich—for a bar, I mean," said Alice.

"Yeah," I replied. "I tried the pizza slices once last month, but they're just some frozen stuff they get from a grocery store. But Wes told me they did sandwiches from scratch, so I thought we could try them out. They don't skimp on anything, do they?"

"Not at all," said Alice. "This thing is huge! You want that dill pickle spear?"

"Hell yeah, I want that pickle!" I laughed and took a bit out of it to stake my claim.

"Which one is Wes? The guitar player?"

"Nah, the guy at the mixing board," I said. "He just graduated High School a month or two ago, and already he's making a name for himself as the go-to sound guy for all the bands in town. That boy is going places."

"He looks too young to be in a club," said Alice. "Not even drinking age yet."

"Might not be," I said. "I notice he's got a co-cola instead of a beer there in front of him. Nice kid, though. Very professional. All the bands I work for tell me he's magic with a mixing board. They're spreading the word he's the guy they all want to make their sound come out the way they want it to be."

The band started playing about then. We swayed back and forth to the music as we sat at the table and finished dinner, then got up and danced a few times during the rest of the night. I should have known it was too good to last, though.

Around midnight, I saw Hassan at the bar. As usual, he was trying to pick up some chick. She wasn't having any of it, though. Just to be safe, I did a quick scan of the crowd and sure enough, some guy was looking angry and getting up to go over and confront Hassan.

"Shit," I said. "Look Alice, I gotta go stop a fight—if I can."

"What? Why? You're not a bouncer here too, are you?"

"No, but I know that guy," I said as I got up.

"Which one?" Alice asked.

"The Arab-looking guy at the bar. The one chasing that skirt. The girl's boyfriend is gonna smack Hassan upside the head for flirting with his girl. Gonna cause trouble—"

"For the band?" Alice asked.

"Trouble for a lot of people," I said. "Hassan's daddy is a king of some sand dune over in the Middle East. I gotta do this, OK?"

"Ride 'em, Cowboy," said Alice. "Go be a big damn hero."

I shot her a sharp look—she sounded pissed off—but I headed for the bar anyway.

I reached the bar just a step or two ahead of the college boy and grabbed Hassan's arm. "Let's take this outside, Hassan," I said. I started moving him along towards the door to the parking lot outside.

Hassan wasn't any too happy with me, but he saw the boyfriend still headed our way and decided to cooperate. I managed to get us outside, but the kid and two of his friends were only a few steps behind us.

"Hey!' he said. "Come back here! I'm gonna whoop your greasy little ass, you bastard."

I gave Hassan a push towards the parking lot. "Run," I told him.

The guy and his buddies caught up with us then. The boyfriend shoved me out of the way and grabbed Hassan's pretty silk shirt, drawing back for a punch. The sidekicks grabbed my arms to keep me out of it—and my training kicked in…

I caught the one on my right with the heel of my shoe to his shin, then stomped down on his foot. He let go of my arm, giving me the chance to sink my right fist into the other guy's solar plexus. He doubled up like a wet wash rag—letting go of my left arm. I spun around and caught the first guy behind the ear with my fist. He went down like a sack of potatoes. The boyfriend was still mouthing threats at Hassan, but hadn't thrown his punch yet. I took three quick steps and dropped down for a leg sweep. That didn't work any too well because the guy was built like a linebacker, but it got the boyfriend off balance long enough for me to straighten up and pop him in the jaw as he turned to deal with me. Must have had a glass jaw, 'cause he was out like a light. I shook my hand to try and take the sting out of my knuckles. A chin is damned *hard,* and punching someone there hurts like hell. Two down and one too busy puking his guts out to be a problem—for now. I grabbed Hassan's arm and started hustling him out deeper into the shadows in the parking lot.

"You *idiot,*" I hissed at him. "Now you've got *five* people mad at you!"

"Five?" Hassan said, stupidly.

"Yeah," I said. "Those three, my girlfriend, and *I'm* none too happy with you at the moment!"

"But—"

"Shut *up!* Find your damn car and get the hell out of here," I said. "Before you cause even *more* trouble."

"Why did you help me?" Hassan asked.

"Because, in spite of the fact you're a womanizing asshole, I kinda *like* you. You don't *mean* any harm, but you keep getting into trouble. Look, just stop trying to pick up girls that already have boyfriends, and we'll *both be* a lot better off. Just get back to your rooms and stay there 'til tomorrow. I don't think these guys got a good enough look at me to recognize me later, so I'm gonna sneak back around front and get back to work—I'm with the band."

"I will do as you ask," said Hassan. "I am in your debt."

"No, you're not," I said. "I'm just doing the right thing because that's what I do. Now, go on—*get!*"

Hassan hurried off—not running, but not dawdling, either. I stuck to the shadows and circled back to the front of the club. I got lucky and the bouncer at the door remembered me from the roadies, so I didn't get hassled getting back in. Alice was still at our table. She wasn't happy with me, but she hid it pretty well for the rest of the night. Once the band's show was over, she left for home.

I didn't get a kiss—just in case you were wondering. I helped the band get packed up and back to their place. The rest of the crew and I unloaded the van and truck. I got paid, then got in my pick-up to head for Alice's house. We didn't argue, but there was a blanket and pillow on the couch when I got there. I took the hint. She was gone to work before I woke up the next day.

I checked the local papers, but the college guys didn't seem to have filed a police report about the fight. Neither did the club, or anyone else for that matter. I drove out to the garage and reported the whole thing to Clay. He didn't like it either, but he knew I did the right thing.

Alice was talking to me again by the time she got home from work that evening. The band had a gig in Atlanta that night, so when the manager called me, I begged off—claiming I'd got some sort of stomach bug. That was an easy cash payment I missed out on, but making up with Alice was more important. Looking back, I believe that was the night our relationship began to cool off.

So far, I thought to myself sarcastically, *retirement is going swimmingly…*

The next time I ran into Hassan, he seemed to have his act together much better. He'd hooked up with a pretty girl from South Georgia whose daddy had made a fortune growing Vidalia onions on a huge farm down there. They'd met in one of their classes, I gathered. In the couple of weeks since the fight at the club, he'd taken time out to rethink his lifestyle a little. The farm-girl was a good influence on him. He wasn't anywhere near as arrogant as he used to be, for one thing, and he seemed happier. We had a little conversation while his new girlfriend was off to powder her nose—or whatever it is that girls do in the Ladies Room—one night at a *different* club, downtown.

"I believe she is the girl of my dreams," he said.

"If you want to keep her," I said, "you better treat her right. If she catches you fooling around with some other women—"

"I will wind up as fertilizer in an onion field on her father's farm," he replied. "This she has made *abundantly* clear to me. She is spirited, this one, exactly what I need."

"Good," I said. "Make sure you keep that in mind."

"We will graduate next year," he said. "She has consented to marry me once we have our diplomas in hand. I shall make her a Queen. She will give my little country exactly the 'shake-up' it has needed for far too long. The traditions have become a hindrance to real progress. I can see that now. High time we climbed out of the 18th-century rut we've been in, and joined the rest of the world in the 20th. I would invite you to the wedding, if I may be so bold."

"That's a long time away from now," I said. "I'll keep it in mind, but I can't make any promises. Are you planning for it to be here, or back home?"

"Here would be best. I want to present my father and my family with a *fait acompli,* as it were," Hassan said.

"Might be best at that," I said. "Might *just* be for the best..."

Alice and I didn't have an easy time of it, ourselves. She went through a rough patch with her teaching job, but managed to keep from having to move away to a different college. Clay kept giving me little jobs, too—so I wasn't always there for her when she needed me. I won't say we were drifting apart, but things did get strained between us for a while. We argued more, for one thing, but we always managed to make up afterwards. The stress was building, nevertheless.

Alice was asked to go to Italy with some of the other Art teachers and a group of students. I fell into keeping her house—our house—in Colbert up while she was away. I got my bike out of storage and started back taking little road trips while she was gone. Just off to little places not too far away, but still fun little day-trips all the same…

Once Alice came back from Europe, we settled into a little routine, but the stress was still there. The university wanted more from her. Clay wanted more from me, too. Finally, she began to complain that I was spending too much time away on my little "side-jobs," as she called them. She didn't know about Clay, or my past as a spy for that matter, but life was conspiring against us all the same.

The tension kept building. The painting and carpentry jobs I'd gotten used to having? Those started drying up. The offers of little gigs helping the local bands set up? Those became fewer and fewer once the bands became more successful. I'd made it clear that I wasn't up for going on tours with any of them. I didn't really need that money. I mean, I made enough from my retirement accounts to live on Easy Street for the rest of my life. Not rich, by any means, but comfortable all the same. Alice wanted to get married, but she was worried that I'd become a "kept man" and get bored with life with her, living off of her income, instead of being the independent guy she'd fallen in love with. I'd reached the point where keeping my past life secret was more and more of an annoyance. I knew I couldn't tell Alice about my past. I knew that the only thing keeping us safe was any enemies I'd once made still thinking I was dead. The other me, I mean. The past me— the spy me.

Weeks would go by, and we did argue from time to time, but not anything like what I'd seen other couples go through. No domestic violence, I mean, just the occasional shouting match. Those didn't last long at the time. We always made up afterwards. But the cracks were beginning to appear.

It didn't help matters that I started going on road trips just to get out of the house when there wasn't any work for me with the contractors or the local bands. I resented having to make Alice think I was dependent on her teaching salary. I mean, I did have enough coming in from my retirement money, so I wasn't poor. But I couldn't show it off, either. I had to continue to look like my construction jobs were my only income. Being audited by the IRS would have blown my cover—brought me back out of the comfortable obscurity that I'd come to treasure—as well as put Alice's life in danger. All it would take was for just *one* of the people I'd crossed in my past life to find out I was still alive. That would be a disaster. Those folks have long memories. They also have short tempers. It didn't help that they had long arms, too. If my cover got blown, someone would come after me with murder on their minds. I was worried that Alice would wind up in the crossfire. I'd die if anything happened to her.

I couldn't see any way out other than to keep my head down and keep hiding in plain sight. Then a guy I'd met a few times around town got a spotlight thrown on himself.

He was a local businessman. An up and comer. He wanted to make it big with his restaurant businesses—but he had a rival. Another restaurant owner with a nice club down at what used to be the local railroad depot. Both of them had restaurants down there—competing with one another. There was bad blood between the two of them. They started trying to sabotage each other's new projects. Nothing violent, just word of mouth, putting investors off of wanting to deal with one or the other. The bad blood got hotter and hotter between them.

Then the murder happened.

The guy I knew, if only tangentially—the restaurant owner I mean—hired another guy I'd met a few times on painting jobs around town, to murder the rival restaurant owner. The hired killer wasn't a pro, by any means, and wasn't able to keep his mouth shut after the murder. He got caught and charged fairly quickly. He then rolled over on the guy that had hired him. So, they both got charged, naturally, and both went to trial. Both of them eventually wound up in prison. In the process, people who happened to know both of them wound up in the fringes of the investigation's spotlight. People like me, I mean, and my fellow construction contract workers around town. I didn't know either of the killers well enough to actually be interviewed by the police, but nonetheless, Clay pitched a right *royal* fit over the possibility of my cover being blown if I were to be called in by the cops to make a statement. I mean, I only knew them well enough to call them by name if I met them on the street. The painter who did the murder I *had* worked with on a couple of jobs around town. And I *had* talked to the businessman who'd contracted the murder about doing some carpentry in a new bar he wanted to open. Matter of fact, it was the dead businessman's blocking the purchase of the building the guilty businessman wanted for that bar—that was what prompted the murder in the first place. I mean, it wasn't outside the realm of possibility that the cops might have asked me for a statement. I didn't know anything beforehand, so it wouldn't have helped them out any.

Clay advised me to lay low, but not leave town, and not do anything to call attention to myself. So that's exactly what I did. I acted as I normally would. I took what few contracting jobs and roadie gigs that were offered to me. I stuck close to home when I wasn't working. If any one asked me about the trial, the murder, or the two guys involved, I played stupid.

Even if it was Alice doing the asking. She knew that I knew both of the killers. I made the mistake of admitting that to her when the news first hit the local papers. She asked me about it more than a few times while the trial was going on.

One night, my nerves were frayed. Alice and I had another argument. We shouted at each other—again. I stormed out of the house, got on my bike, and took off to ride the back roads around Colbert to clear my head. I was going too fast, I admit. I was distracted—I'll admit that too. I was mad at myself, mad at Alice, mad that we'd been arguing—just generally mad at the world. Madder at myself that I'd let my life get into such a mess. But the night was dark, the road was there, the bike was loud, and the ride was helping clear my head. I took the next curve as fast as I dared, then opened the bike up again on the straightaway.

I must have gotten the old Harley up to seventy or thereabouts when I hit the flying saucer...

To Be Continued in:

"Abducted!" by Dan L. Hollifield, Published by Three Ravens Publishing

We hope that you enjoyed this title and look forward to many more to come. Please, leave us a review! Reviews matter to all of our authors.

Take a look at some of our other award-winning series at https://threeravenspublishing.com/series-universes/

Visit us at https://www.threeravenspublishing.com and sign up for our newsletter for the latest and greatest news on upcoming titles and events.

Other series and titles you might enjoy.

JOINT TASK FORCE 13
AVAILABLE ON
AMAZON
HOLDING THE LINE
BETWEEN HEAVEN AND HELL
13

B.E.N.T.
BIOLOGIC   ENHANCED   NASCENT   TALENT

STARFLIGHT

IT CAME FROM THE
TRAILER PARK

You can also keep up to date with our latest release announcements on <u>Scifi.radio</u> and get some of the best fandom programing on the planet.

Scifi for your Wifi

And don't forget to check out our other Sponsors and Affiliates

A southern Appalachian jewel for craft beer lovers, Buck Bald Brewing offers something for everyone.

To discover more visit us at buckbaldbrewing.com

Revolution X is a testament to the power of collaboration, blending four unique styles into a cohesive, revolutionary sound. When these four individuals unite, the result is nothing short of musical Revolution!

Would you like to learn how to write and market your own titles? The following affiliates links might be helpful.

Don't forget to check out the latest edition of Car Warriors: Autoduel Chronicle fiction series.

Comprised of active or retired servicemen and civilian volunteers, Shepherd's Men enthusiastically raises awareness and funds for the SHARE Military Initiative (SHARE) at Shepherd Center in Atlanta, GA.

This nationally renowned program focuses on assessment and treatment for American military veterans who have sustained mild to moderate Traumatic Brain Injury (TBI) and Post-Traumatic Stress Disorder (PTSD) during post-9/11 service.

Find out more at: https://www.shepherdsmen.com/